Snow's
ADDICTION
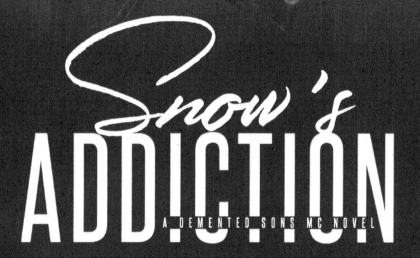

A DEMENTED SONS MC NOVEL

KRISTINE ALLEN

Dedication

To all of you that believe dreams don't come true. I once dreamed of being a published author. Follow your dreams!

Snow's Addiction

They call me Snow.

The Demented Sons MC is my family, and I'm their president.

A short stint in the military after my brother's death taught me discipline, loyalty, and how to kill without remorse. But it did nothing for my guilt.

My brother died because of me and my choices. I didn't deserve to be loved, nor did I want it. Casual sex was enough, because I was married to my grief.

After an out-of-town one-night stand, I began to think I could be wrong. I couldn't get her out of my head. Too bad we'd decided no names. With kids in my town overdosing left and right and a killer on the loose, it was probably for the best.

Then she showed up in my backyard, playing with fire hot enough to burn us all to the ground.

Snow's

ADDICTION

A DEMENTED SONS MC NOVEL

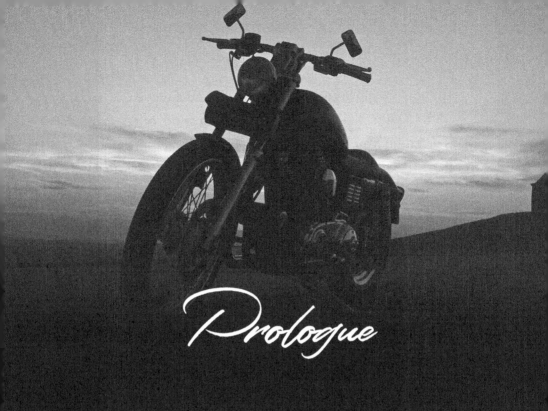

Prologue

Snow

Almost twenty years old…

"**Y**OU WORTHLESS PIECE OF SHIT!" A COWBOY BOOT HIT THE wall next to my head as I ducked. "You're not gonna be livin' under my roof for free. The worst thing I ever did was tell your mother she didn't have to get an abortion! You've been nothing but trouble your whole life!"

Spittle flew each time he spewed a hateful word at me. Not that I wasn't used to it; I'd been told what a sorry excuse for a son I was for as long as I could remember. Everything that went wrong was my fault. I was a disappointment. I ruined his life. I'd heard it all. As if he was father of the year.

It didn't pay to argue with him, so I bit my tongue.

"I told your mother you were up to no good, but she's always defendin' you. Look at the example you're settin' for your brother!" He motioned, and I glanced over my shoulder to see my younger brother standing there white-faced and wide-eyed. I knew it wasn't me that was putting that look on his face. He hated the way our father talked to us. It was part of why he'd started fucking with alcohol and drugs to begin with. "It's no wonder he's a freak with an example like you!"

Granted, I had fucked up. I'd been kicked out of college the day before. My grades had slipped because I was so worried about Leon that I couldn't concentrate. I'd been on scholastic probation when I'd been caught smoking weed with several of my teammates. My lack of focus merely sealed my coffin.

Barely into my sophomore year, I'd been sent home with my tail between my legs, while the other guys had gotten a slap on the wrist. It was bullshit, but I didn't have their grades. I'd been good enough at football to get a scholarship, but when my brother started going off the rails, I fell apart.

"Hey, Leon, go back to your room, okay?" I said it as quietly as I could, but my father still heard.

"He don't take orders from you! You shoulda went to jail where you belong! Then you wouldn't be around to influence him!"

Went to jail? Seriously? For flunking out and smoking weed? My jaw clenched as I fought to hold in the words he deserved.

Leon was nothing like me. With our father's blond hair and a slight build, he was the opposite of my brown hair and bulky frame. Except now, his hair was dyed black with a long flop over

2

his eyes. Thick black liner rimmed his haunted eyes. Happy to sit in his room and play video games, he was a quiet introvert. He'd also been spending a lot of time with the Edwards kid, and I didn't like that. Despite his dad being a cop, the kid was a punk. Leon was a good kid, but I was worried his choice in friends was affecting him in a negative way. Appearing torn, he finally took my advice.

In my mind, I said a word of thanks when he silently went back down the hallway.

"I'm going to work," my father said as he grabbed his jacket and lunch box. "I want your shit packed and you out of my house by the time I get home."

He worked the second shift at the packing plant on the south edge of town. Mom worked at the bank, so she wouldn't be home for an hour or so. I'd figure something out and let her know I was leaving to keep the peace for her and my brother.

"Good riddance," I muttered under my breath as he stormed out the door.

I'd been dreading coming home, but Decker had joined the Army, so I couldn't go stay with him. More than likely, I'd join up too. Maybe we'd get stationed together. The rest of my friends had either moved away or didn't really have room for me, so that wasn't an option either. One was actually in prison, but we hadn't been that close anyway.

Maybe I hadn't been the best kid, but I wasn't that bad. I did all the typical shit—broke a few bones trying to do stunts on my bike and my skateboard, smoked a little weed, experimented with some other shit, drank, but I never brought the law home.

Deciding to chill in my room, I tromped down the hall. My

bedroom door was ajar, and I wondered if Leon had gone to my room to wait. Except he wasn't in there.

Wanting to check on him after our father's rant, I went next door to his room.

When I pushed into the room, my stomach bottomed out.

Leon was sprawled on the floor.

I dropped to my knees and shook him. "Leon!"

When he didn't wake up, I tried to see if I could find a pulse, but I didn't know what I was doing. "Shit!"

I dug my flip phone out of my pocket and called 911. That's when I saw the mess on his desk. White powder scattered on the surface with a shortened coffee straw to the side. As the operator asked me what my emergency was, I was diving back to my brother.

"My little brother; I think he overdosed!" I rattled off our address, begging them to hurry. Not having a clue if I did it right, I plugged his nose and blew into his mouth.

"Oh my God, Leon. What did you do?" I cried as I shook him again.

Except I already knew the answer to that. I just didn't understand what possessed my brother to do it and how the hell he'd known where I'd stashed it. As I cradled my little brother's still form, tears poured down my face.

Beating myself up, I begged God to help me.

I'd caught Leon with the shit when I returned home that day. Dad had come home from the gas station, and I didn't have a chance to dispose of it, so I shoved it in my pillowcase. If only I hadn't panicked. If only I'd disposed of it immediately, this wouldn't have happened.

4

Why? Why hadn't I flushed it?

The EMS crew rushed into the house, and I got out of the way. As the paramedics worked on him, I fell back on my ass. Leaning against the bed in shock, I looked up as my mother burst into the room. The police officer who'd shown up with the ambulance grabbed her. She was screaming and crying as she fought to get to my brother.

"My baby! Oh my God, my baby! Let me go!" she sobbed.

Stunned disbelief overwhelmed me, and I struggled to breathe. Then I told myself I didn't deserve to if Leon couldn't. This was all my fault. My father was right. I was a fuckup.

When they loaded him up in the ambulance, they took off without sirens, and I knew.

My mother had insisted on riding with him because I think she held out hope. I had none.

"Son, do you know anything about where your brother got the cocaine?" the older officer asked me. There was no way they would believe me if I told them the truth. Especially not that officer. Lifting my head, I met his concerned gaze and condemned myself to hell.

"I have no idea."

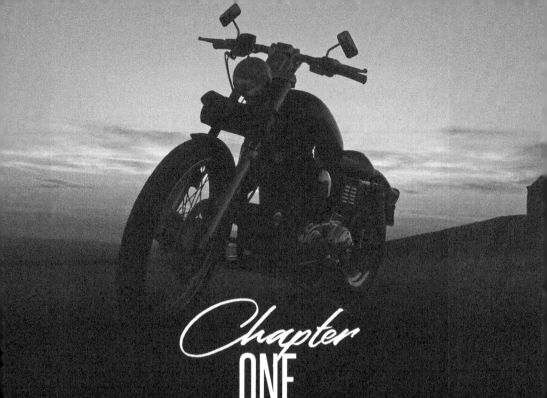

Chapter ONE

Snow

"I'M NOT OKAY (I PROMISE)"—MY CHEMICAL ROMANCE

Age 37...

"H EY, P. I HEARD CAMMIE PACKED HER SHIT AND LEFT town," Reaper said as he sat at the bar next to me. He motioned to the bartender for a beer.

"Mm," I grunted, not wanting to talk about it.

Cammie and I had a good thing going for a while. We'd warmed each other's beds, and there were no strings attached. At least, there weren't until the day there were. It turned out she wanted more from me than I was willing to give. When I told

Cammie she was getting everything she'd ever get from me, she'd packed her shit and said she was moving to Oregon.

Guess she did.

"You okay?" he asked.

"What is this, a counseling session? We gonna sit down and discuss our feelings?" I gruffly questioned.

Sure, I missed her, but it didn't break my heart. Then again, it couldn't, because I was pretty sure I didn't have one anymore. At least not when it came to women. My club? My brothers? They had whatever part of my heart still existed.

Maybe that made me a cold bastard, but fuck it.

Joker elbowed Reaper, who glared at him. Like I wouldn't notice. There was little that escaped my attention. They spoke quietly, and I chose to ignore them.

"How much longer you gonna be here?" Reaper asked. I shrugged.

"It's still early, but don't stay on my account. No one knows us here. I'll be okay," I told the boys. We were on our way home from Texas for Gunny's wedding and had stopped for the night in Kansas. Still kind of ate at me that I lost both Lock and Gunny to the Central Texas chapter, but I understood why Lock needed to get away. Then, once their whole family moved, it only made sense that Gunny would follow.

"Yeah, and then if things do go south, I'll feel like a fucking piece of shit. No way. Not leaving my prez alone." Reaper was staring at me with narrowed eyes. "Besides, I need to finish my beer."

He raised the bottle in a mock salute with a cocky grin.

Shaking my head, I rolled my eyes. To appease them, I finished my drink. "Well, bottoms up. I'm done."

Reaper and Joker both gave me a deadpan stare that screamed a sarcastic "Really?" Reaper blinked in irritation, and Joker chewed on the toothpick he kept in his mouth. He'd quit smoking a while back, and if he was around alcohol, he needed something to keep him from wanting to light up. I laughed and stood from my seat.

Tossing a twenty on the bar, I headed to the door. The scrape of stools behind me echoed through the small bar over the sound of the raggedy-ass jukebox they had. The one Gunny had was a hell of a lot better.

"Sometimes you're a real dick," Reaper grumbled.

"Most men would get their teeth knocked out for saying that," I said as I raised a brow.

Again with the cocky grin, he said, "Guess it's a good thing I'm not most men."

I snorted as we walked outside and next door to our motel. Using the old-fashioned brass key, I opened my door. "You boys sleep tight. No hanky-panky tonight."

They both shot me the bird before entering their room, laughing. I closed my door and sat on the edge of the bed. Both Reaper and Joker had ol' ladies, so I wasn't going to make them hang out in a bar with me all damn night, but I wasn't fucking tired.

Figured I'd wait a bit, then head back next door. We weren't in a hurry to leave in the morning, so I could sleep in. Tonight, I simply needed to drink away some ghosts.

Alone.

After about thirty minutes of surfing through my phone and replying to messages from my buddy Venom and then my VP,

Vinny, I sent a text to my mom so she wouldn't worry. I wasn't overly concerned about shit at home. Vinny was solid—I knew he had things covered.

"No issues?" I asked when Vinny called. He wasn't much for texting, so I wasn't surprised.

"Depends on how you look at it," he hedged.

"Explain," I demanded, and he sighed.

"There was an overdose tonight. Some kid from over in Spirit Lake, but it happened here at his cousin's place."

"Fuck. Do we know what it was or where he got it?"

"That's the weird thing. They don't know what the hell it was."

"What the fuck you mean, they don't know what it was?"

"Rumor has it there is a new drug making the rounds, but I didn't realize it was in our area. They think it may be that, but they aren't releasing details from toxicology and shit." I could hear the tension in his tone. He and the rest of my club had the same stance on drugs. They were an absolute no go. Weed, sure; anything else—hard pass.

"Jesus Christ. Well, see what you can find out. Have Hacker look into it too. We'll be home early tomorrow evening."

"Roger that. Let me know when you all hit the road."

"Will do," I assured him before ending the call. When I found out who was peddling shit to kids in my area, they were going to wish they'd never been born.

I needed to take a piss, then I needed another drink. Preferably a double.

Once I finished my business, I washed up and stared hard in the mirror. What I saw made me despise myself a little. The older I got, the more I looked like my old man. Except, after my brother died, he not only abused drugs, he drank himself into an early grave, so who knew what he'd look like by now. Good riddance. He'd been part of the reason Leon and I had fucked with drugs in the first place.

It's true what they say. Sometimes you live what you learn.

Though, unlike our father, Leon and I had only smoked weed while we both lived under that roof. I'd had no idea he'd moved on to other things while I was away at college.

Shaking off the melancholy thoughts, I decided it had been long enough. Quietly, I let myself out of the room. The temperature had dropped in the short time since I'd walked back to the motel. It wasn't unbearable, but I could've used a jacket. To ward off the chill, I shoved my hands in my jeans pockets and moved faster.

The place had picked up a little since I'd left. Spotting two open stools at the bar, I beelined over and sat down.

"Back so soon?" the bartender asked me with a good-natured grin. I lifted a shoulder.

"Yeah, couldn't sleep."

"Same?" he asked, and I nodded. In no time, he set the glass in front of me. I took a sip and lost myself in the amber liquid for a minute. Memories and regrets sifted through my head.

"Is this seat taken?" a woman asked at my side, and I glanced over.

Goddamn.

"Nope," I said, unable to take my eyes off her. The woman sat down, dressed in a tight red dress with matching heels. Bit much for this area of town, if you asked me, but hell if I was complaining. My eyes wandered to her long legs.

"Thanks," she said once she was settled, and I pulled my eyes up to her face. She flashed me a subdued smile, and my dick woke up as her deep red lips curled. Eyes so pale they appeared silver caught mine briefly before she turned to place her order with the bartender.

Her drink sat in front of her untouched for several minutes. Curious, I glanced her way and studied her profile. Dark honey hair was tucked behind her ear, and a small diamond winked on her lobe.

"You seem awfully dressed up for this place." I'd told myself I wasn't going to engage, but something about her drew me in. She snorted a laugh.

"Well, I was trying to go out and have a good time tonight, but my friends are either married with kids to get home to, or they hooked up with someone and ditched me."

"So you came here?" I chuckled. She bit her lip, then gave me a quick sidelong glance.

"Yeah. My sister and I used to sneak in here before we turned twenty-one."

"So why isn't she out with you tonight?"

"She's dead."

"Oh, shit, I'm sorry."

"It's okay. You didn't know." She paused and took a drink. "Today, it's been five years."

"I'm really sorry, but I understand. It's been seventeen years since my baby brother died."

"I'm sorry, too. Do you mind my asking what happened?"

I sighed and rubbed my chest at the pain the memory caused.

"Drug overdose. Hard to believe he would've been thirty-two this year."

"Jesus. I get it, though. My sister also died from a drug overdose. I'd tried for years to get her sober, but every time she'd get clean, she slipped, until the last slip cost her everything." A tear escaped her eye, and she quickly wiped it away. "Sorry. I'm a bit of a buzzkill."

"Naw, it's okay. I feel you." This week had been the anniversary of my brother's death as well. I'd welcomed the trip to get my mind off it. Except it caught up with me anyway.

"You from around here?" she asked me.

"Nope. Passing through."

She nodded, and we returned our attention to our drinks.

After my next one and the start of her second, I sent a quick glance her way. "So, you grew up around here?"

I really tried not to engage further, but it was impossible. She was entirely too beautiful for this run-down dive. Too classy for me, too, but it didn't stop me from drinking her in as I waited for her answer.

"Yeah. Kansas girl. When I was young, I always wished we'd moved over to the Missouri side of Kansas City, but my parents wouldn't leave here. As soon as I could, I hauled ass across the river." She gave a crooked grin that made my chest ripple and my dick twitch.

"Yet you're back here now."

She laughed humorlessly as she peeked at me from the corner of her eye. "It would appear so."

"Why? Because you used to come here with your sister? Surely there are nicer places you could've gone to over there."

Her shoulders rose slightly before drooping. A moment later, her chin appeared to quiver.

In an attempt to lighten the mood, because I felt for her, I teased, "So you wanna fight, fuck, or throw rocks?"

Her silver eyes locked on me. Intrigued, I stared as they looked me over, pausing slightly at my lips before moving down. They snapped back to mine, then she downed the rest of her drink and stood.

Well, that backfired.

"You got a room?" Her no-nonsense tone and question caught me by surprise.

"Yeah, next door." Warily, I watched her.

"Let's fuck."

The guy next to me choked on his drink, and I threw enough money on the scarred-up wood to cover both our drinks. Not wanting to wait for her to change her mind, I stood and gently grabbed the bend of her elbow. Then I paused, because I wasn't a complete asshole.

"You serious?"

"As a goddamn heart attack. Let's go." She started to walk, and I either had to keep up or let go. I sure as fuck wasn't letting go.

The wind ruffled her wavy hair as we exited the building, and the flowery scent of it hit me. She casually tucked it behind her ear again.

"This way." I guided her, trying to ignore the obvious peaks of her nipples through the tight red dress. Christ almighty, I was damn near ready to bust a nut in my jeans.

As quietly as I could, I opened my door and ushered her in.

I'd barely gotten it closed when she had me pressed against the cool metal.

"Where are you from?" she asked as she ran a lacquered nail along my bottom lip.

"Does it matter?"

Her brow rose, then she smirked. "No, not really."

"Good." I tugged my T-shirt off and tossed it on the chair. Before I could get to my buckle, her hands were working it loose. When she dropped to her knees in front of me, I grinned, then hissed as she freed my cock.

She gripped the base tightly, pumped it a few times, then ran her tongue around the tip, and I almost swallowed my goddamn tongue. "Jesus fucking tits," I gasped when she wrapped those ruby lips around my girth. My eyes rolled back in my head. Then she worked me over like nobody's business.

At thirty-seven years old, I was no inexperienced kid, but holy hell, she gave the best blow job I'd had in my entire damn life. My fingers tangled in her silken tresses as my eyes rolled back. Before I could really corral my thoughts, I was on the verge of shooting my shit down her lily-white throat.

Digging my hands in and tugging, I pulled her off my dick with a *pop*. Disappointment registered in her eyes until I demanded, "Take off that dress or it's gonna end up in two pieces, then get your sweet ass on the bed."

Passion heavy in her eyes, she stood defiantly in front of me and slowly peeled the dress from her body. Standing before me in a red thong and those red fuck-me heels, she shook out her golden locks.

With a growl, I lifted her by the waist, and she wrapped her legs tightly around my hips.

My teeth grazed her neck as I approached the bed. A soft mewling came from deep in her throat. The scent she wore was driving me crazy.

When I reached the edge of the mattress, I laid her down and crawled between her long legs. They spread further to accommodate me. As I rested on my elbows, one arm under her, hand clutching her hair, I tasted her everywhere I could reach.

"Yes," she murmured as I circled her nipple with my tongue before drawing it into my mouth to suckle it. Not wanting the other to feel left out, I plucked at it with my fingers. She was utterly exquisite—the perfect distraction from my earlier melancholy thoughts.

As I worked my way down her stomach, she arched her hips up, seeking friction I wasn't going to give yet. Sitting back on my heels, I raised one shapely leg. A kiss to her ankle, then I removed the first shoe, trailing kisses up to the sensitive area behind her knee. When I'd covered every inch with either kisses or caresses, I moved over to the other one.

Repeating my movements on that limb, I worked my way up to the lace of her panties. "I can smell you," I groaned against her inner thigh. My beard must've tickled her, because goose bumps skated across her skin, and her legs trembled.

"God, please," she begged.

"Please what?" I whispered, wanting to hear her say what she wanted. Mesmerized by her, I skimmed my rough hands along the generous curves of her silken skin. Not a single part of her was left untouched. My eyes held hers as she panted with need below me.

"Please," she uttered again, but without specifics, I continued to tease her. Finally reaching the apex of her thighs, I licked along either side of the lace before sucking the fabric along with her clit into my mouth. She let out a low moan as her fingers clutched my hair. Shamelessly, she ground her pussy into my face.

If I was going to suffocate in her, it sure as hell wasn't going to be with a scrap of fabric between us. I reached up and ripped them on one side, then the other before throwing them to the floor.

Bared to my torture, her cunt wept for me. I gathered the liquid on my lips and tongue and slid two fingers into her tight heat. I paused long enough to demand, "What do you want?"

"Make me come," she pleadingly whispered. My lips curled into a wicked grin.

"With pleasure," I murmured before diving back in. Relentless, I drove her over the edge for the first time. If I had my way, there would be many more before I was done.

"Oh my fuck! Holy shit!" She thrashed and gasped, trying to jerk away from my skillful ministrations, but I didn't let up. I owned her—at least for the night.

When her spasms slowed to an occasional flutter, I licked her essence from my fingers. Her breathing sped up as I braced myself on my arms and hovered above her. Barely touching, I licked the soft, plush skin of her lips. Then I kissed her, allowing her to taste the intoxicating flavor of her release on my tongue.

Her nails dug into me as she returned my kiss with wild abandon.

Longing consumed me as I gently bit her before pulling away. Needing to be inside her, I dug in my pocket before I stripped out of my remaining clothes. With sure movements, I sheathed my painfully hard cock and settled the tip against her wet core.

"I'm going to fuck you so hard you'll feel this night for days and you'll remember it for the rest of your life." Her eyes widened, and lust filled their silvery depths. Satisfaction gleamed in her heated gaze.

Teasingly, I swirled the tip and took a few shallow dips into her soaking wet pussy before I thrust hard, seating myself to the hilt. She gasped, and I groaned as she tightened unbelievably around my shaft. I swear to fucking Christ, I'd never experienced something so amazing.

"Jesus," I rasped out as I held myself still above her. Once I was sure I wouldn't blow my load in the first few seconds, I pushed her thighs to her chest and rested her shins against my body. "Hang on, baby."

Chapter
TWO

Snow

"STILL BREATHING"—GREEN DAY

A S WE PULLED ON OUR GLOVES AND HELMETS, REAPER AND Joker both glared at me. Neither of them said a word, but they continued to shoot daggers at me as we prepared to hit the road.

"What?" I finally asked them, exasperated.

"You kept us up all goddamn night," Reaper muttered. Joker smirked but tried to hide it by dropping his gaze to the ground.

"What the fuck are you talking about?" I questioned, though I knew.

"I need to get some coffee at the gas station. Thanks to your wall-banging, I didn't sleep for shit," Reaper grumbled as he shoved his phone into the faring compartment.

"Pretty sure we got screwed, and I didn't even get my dick wet," Joker added as he snickered.

"You have an ol' lady," I deadpanned.

"Hey, I didn't say I would've wanted to cheat. Sera is definitely my one and only. I just said my dick didn't get wet," Joker replied with a shrug. Reaper shook his head at Joker's antics.

"Didn't know you had it in you, old man. That bed damn near came through the wall," Joker said with a snicker.

"Old man? Who the actual fuck are you calling an old man?" I growled with a frown as I sat on my bike. They waited until I was mounted up before they did.

"Well, with all that gray in your beard," Reaper replied with a chuckle. Joker slid his shades on and tried not to laugh. My blood boiled a little. I wasn't fucking old.

"Fuck. You. My beard started to go gray when I was thirty. I can't fucking help genetics. But last time I checked, thirty-seven wasn't old. And I can assure you, she had no complaints." Ending the conversation, I drowned out their laughter by starting my bike and twisting the throttle. They followed suit, and we pulled out of the lot.

As the miles slipped away, I admitted to myself that part of the reason I was in such a shitty mood was because the chick from last night was gone when I woke up. Not that I expected anything lasting, but one for the road would've been nice.

All the way home to Grantsville, I replayed the night before. It was completely and totally worth the lack of sleep. Everything about her was perfect—and I didn't mean her looks, though they were too.

The fact that she was feisty, yet a little broken. The way she boldly met my every demand. Not once did she shy away from what I gave her. She reveled in it and met me move for move. It was probably the best fuck I'd had in a long time. Usually, women tried every trick in the book to fuck me so they had bragging rights. They all wanted to be able to say they did the president of the Demented Sons. While they tried, I'd been loyal to Cammie when we were sleeping together. Last night's chick didn't know who I was and wanted me for me—it was fucking amazing.

Regardless, it was probably best I hadn't gotten the woman's name or number. Because I swear to Christ, I would've been tempted to make the six-hour trip for another round with her. My dick was rousing at the thought.

I fought it the entire way home.

Backing my bike up to the clubhouse, I breathed a sigh of relief. It had been a long ride with too much caffeine consumed, and it was good to be home. Too bad I still had trouble brewing.

No rest for the weary and wicked.

"Snow, how was the trip?" Vinny asked the second I entered the dimly lit clubhouse.

"Long. I want a sitrep ASAP. Call church in one hour. I need to wash the road grime off my ass." Vinny nodded, and I went straight to my room.

The hot water beating down on my back did nothing to relax my knotted muscles. Shoving my face in the stream, I stood there until I couldn't hold my breath any longer. Both hands scrubbed my face and shoved my hair back.

A flash in my mind of a fiery vixen on her knees before me had my dick going hard as a rock. Remembering every second of what she'd done, I stroked my length in a tight grip. Eyes closed, I saw her ruby-red lips stretched around me as she took me as deep as she could.

Before I knew it, I was shooting jets of cum on the shower floor, where it washed down the drain. A shudder shook me as I squeezed my cock one last time, causing me to suck a sharp breath in through my clenched teeth.

"Fucking hell," I said with a ragged breath as I pressed my forehead to the cool tiles.

After cleaning up, I dried off and dressed in clean clothes. Brushing my hair and beard, I stared sightlessly toward the mirror. It was fucked up, but I wanted to go back and scour Kansas City for her.

Jesus, I needed to get my head in the game. I was the motherfucking president of the Demented Sons in Iowa. There was no time or room in my head to obsess over some random one-night stand.

Locking my memories of her up in a mental vault, I pulled on my boots and stomped to the chapel. Focusing on my current problem, I sat at the empty table to wait. Whoever was peddling this new shit in my area was a dead man.

"The shit is going by the street name of Black Night. It's a blend of opiates, heroin, and synthetic shit that varies from batch to batch. It's unstable and can be extremely toxic. It can be swallowed, snorted, smoked, or injected—whatever trips the user's trigger. From what I can find, it's being brought in from over on the East Coast, but no one can pinpoint exactly where." Hacker looked up from his laptop after he was done.

"Jesus Christ," muttered Apollo. No one called him DJ anymore. Not since he'd been patched, anyway. He'd grown up around here, too, only leaving for an enlistment and two overseas tours. This bullshit was personal to him too. This was home.

"No idea who's slinging that shit around here?" I asked, smoothing my beard in frustration.

"The only one we tracked down overdosed right before the kid here did. Shit is no joke." Hollywood slouched back in his chair as he nervously tapped his fingers on the tabletop.

"I want everyone on this. Pull in any of the informants we have. Known junkies from over at the Lakes, here, anyone. If you have an in with the kids in this area, use it. No leaf unturned and all that. Someone has to know something, for fuck's sake," I growled.

We made a plan to divide and conquer. Everyone stood when I ended church and filed out of the chapel. No one stopped at the bar for drinks—we had things to do.

Besides this shitshow with the fucking drugs, I needed to get over to the planning committee meeting for the annual fundraiser at the Leon Adolescent Center. I might be able to talk to a few of the kids there. Most weren't from around here, but some were.

Since spring was finally breaking, I continued to take advantage of riding my bike. We could always have a random winter storm trying to have one last hurrah. I hated that shit, and it was part of the reason I ended up with the road name of "Snow." Hell, maybe *I* was the one who should've moved to Texas.

After parking, I took off my helmet, hung it on my bars, and headed inside.

"Hey, Alba," I drawled with a grin to the receptionist as I leaned my arms on the counter. "Polly busy? I'm a little early."

"I'll check for you, handsome," Alba said, shooting me a wink. She was one of my mother's friends, so I knew she didn't mean anything by it. Growing up, she'd been like a second mom.

"'Preciate it," I replied as I grinned. Lost in thought, I stared out the window.

"Luke. Come on back," Polly called out, causing me to turn to face her. Glancing down, I realized she was using a cane. A concerned frown furrowed my brow.

"You okay, Polly?"

"What—this?" She gestured to the cane. "Just my hip acting up. Doc says I'm gonna need a replacement—that I've put it off too long."

"Anything I can do?"

"Not unless you've secretly discovered the fountain of youth!" she replied in a tone tinged with laughter.

"Unfortunately, I haven't," I said as I pointed at my graying beard. We both laughed at that.

We entered her office and sat. She winced and heaved a deep sigh. The rest of the members of the small committee came in. The next hour was spent going over their budget and the plans for this year's fundraiser. It helped us set a goal.

Once everything was finalized, everyone but Polly and I left the office.

"Luke, we sure do appreciate what you boys do for this facility. Without the money you raise every year, we wouldn't be able to do half the things we do for these kids. State funding isn't what people think it is, and we try to keep the costs down for the families that don't have great insurance—or no insurance. You boys not only helped this place get off the ground, you've been here for us every step of the way." The kind look in her eyes made me fidget a little in my seat. Praise made me uncomfortable, because in a way, keeping this place running was not only a pleasure, it was a penance.

My gaze dropped to where I was absently spinning one of my rings.

"Luke," she said softly, "what happened to Leon wasn't your fault. You didn't force the drugs on him. You tried to stop him, but you were essentially a kid yourself. I really do appreciate what your club does for us, but you don't owe anyone anything."

With a sharp inhale and a slow, shaky exhale, I tried to meet her eyes. I wasn't a goddamn coward, but some things were difficult to accept. My brother's death not being my fault was one of them.

"We'll have to agree to disagree on that," I said with a failed attempt at a smile. She was one of the only ones who knew my truth, because she'd found me that awful day. I'd broken down after my brother's funeral. Staring at the cloudy sky, I'd been sprawled in a field on the edge of town between her place and ours, a pistol in my hand. How she'd seen me out there, I hadn't a clue.

She might've convinced me to talk to her, but I'd drawn the line at counseling. Counseling was out of the question, because they'd want me to talk about what happened. I was weak. I'd break. And I refused to look weak in front of my father.

Instead, trying to outrun my ghosts, I'd joined the Army like my friend Decker had—praying with each deployment I didn't make it home. I got out after Mom told me Dad had drunk himself into an early grave. He was a verbally and mentally abusive, hateful bastard anyway, but Mom had loved him. Maybe he didn't lay a hand on us, but he still did a number on us all.

"Luke," she started. I held up a hand.

After joining the Demented Sons, I made it my goal to get the adolescent facility built. Then I convinced the club to do annual fundraisers. For the DSMC, it gave them a sense of legitimacy and made them look better to the community.

Back then, we'd been hypocritical as fuck, because we were one of the main suppliers to the surrounding areas. Part of the reason I'd joined the club was to try to get them to stop. When I moved up the ranks, I pushed and slowly cleaned up our act. Sure, we still had our fingers in a lot of shit, but I'd eradicated the sale of drugs in the chapter. It was too little, too late, but I'd laid down the law.

Now it seemed we had our work cut out for us. If I could help it, no more kids would die of drug overdoses. At least not on my watch.

I stood.

"I really need to get to the shop. Anything else we need to finalize before I go?"

Sad eyes and an equally sad smile were trained on me. When she stood to show me out, she struggled, and I rushed behind the desk to help her. She sighed. "Don't tell anyone, because I haven't announced it yet, but this will be the last fundraiser I do."

Taken by surprise, I cocked my head and frowned in confusion. "What are you talking about?"

"It's time for me to retire. I'm tired. Not that I don't enjoy my job—it's been amazingly fulfilling. But it's time." She shrugged, then shooed me toward the door before putting weight on the cane.

"Well, I'm sorry that I won't be working with you anymore after this year, but if you ever need anything, you know you can call me, right? Oh, and try not to hire a replacement that's a pain in the ass to work with." I chuckled.

"No assholes. Noted," she said as she made a mock checkmark in the air. "Don't worry; it's going to take several months for me to get my paperwork submitted and someone else through the hiring process."

We laughed as she walked me out into the lobby.

"If anything changes or you need anything before the event, you let me know," I firmly insisted.

She gripped my arm and slid her hand down to hold mine in a way that conveyed love, emotion, and support that I didn't feel I deserved. "You know we will," she murmured with a small, resigned smile.

"You care if I visit with some of the kids before I go?" I asked Polly.

"Feel free. They should be between groups right now," she replied with a smile.

As I backed away from the counter, I slid on my shades and waved to Polly and Alba.

I stepped out into the sunshine, completely unaware that what she'd told me was going to change my life irrevocably.

Chapter THREE

Hailey

"DEAR LIFE"—HIGH VALLEY

One year later...

A S I SAT ACROSS THE TABLE FROM MY DATE, A BLAND SMILE pasted on my face, my mind wandered. The words he was rambling, extolling his awesomeness, faded away. What a shitty date it had turned out to be.

A flashback of the night with the sexy stranger played through my head like a home movie—if that movie was in 3D. Every move he'd made had been magic. Hot, sweaty, pulse-pounding magic.

When he'd told me I wouldn't ever forget that night, he wasn't kidding. I've literally relived it every single night since. In vivid technicolor.

"So when I finished up, everyone was coming over to congratulate me," my date said. What the hell was his name again? Charlie? Chester? Wait. No, it was Chet. And what the hell was he talking about?

"That's awesome," I said as I pasted a brilliant fake smile on my face. I was going to choke my new friend Justine for setting this up. While he was good-looking, he was at the top of the douche pyramid. Numero Uno in the douche-canoe parade.

With a pleased grin, he raised his glass for a drink. Unable to handle another minute, I frowned and made a production of pulling out my phone. Looking at the blank screen, I whispered, "Oh, shoot."

"Is everything okay?" he asked with a furrowed brow.

"It's my mother. She says it's important that I call. I'll just be a minute," I said as I excused myself to step outside. Then I held the phone to my ear and had a one-way conversation with no one. After an acceptable amount of time had passed, I reentered the restaurant. Then I slapped a worried expression on my face as I approached the table.

"I'm so sorry to cut our night short, but I need to run home. It's my mom. She's visiting, and she thinks she sprained her ankle." With an Oscar-worthy look of concern, I gathered my purse and light jacket.

He placed his napkin on the table and stood. "Is there anything I can do?"

"Oh, no. Thank you, though. That's sweet of you. Thank you

so much for dinner. It was lovely." I blinked a few times and shot him an apologetic smile.

"Let me walk you to your car," he offered. Afraid he might ask me out again on the way or, God forbid, try to kiss me, I waved him off.

"No need, but thank you. You finish your dessert." Before he could say any more, I rushed out, heels clicking on the tiled floors. The sun had gone down, and the temperature had dropped, but I didn't pause to slip my jacket on.

Reaching my car, I was thankful I'd insisted on meeting him at the restaurant that overlooked the lake. Not wasting time, I started the car, cranked up the heat, and got on the road.

The lights of the lake faded in my rearview mirror as I headed home. My phone rang, and I grinned as I saw the display. "Hey, Mom. Your ears must've been burning."

Her chuckle carried over the line. "What are you up to?"

"Oh, not much, just heading home because you might have sprained your ankle," I said, then pulled my lips between my teeth in an attempt not to laugh.

"Child, you are incorrigible. One of these days, you using me as your escape plan from bad dates is gonna backfire. What was wrong with this one?" Her tone was chastising, but the laugh at the end ruined the effect she was going for.

"Ugh, well, let's just say, pretty package but too in love with himself."

"One of those, huh?"

"You have no idea."

"Well, your father and I are talking about making a trip up

to see you. When is a good week?" We ironed out the details, and I pulled into my neighborhood on the edge of town.

"Okay, Mom, I'll see you in a few weeks."

"Sounds good. Maybe while I'm there I can find a nice boy for you. You're not getting any younger, and I sure would love some grandbabies to spoil."

Laughing, I parked in my garage. I didn't bother to tell her I didn't need a man to give her grandbabies. We talked for a few minutes before I wrapped up the conversation. Once I ended the call, I grabbed my crap and went inside.

After dumping everything on the counter and kicking off my shoes, I shuffled to my room and fell back onto my bed.

Then I shot off a text to Justine.

Me: I hate you. We can no longer be friends.

Justine: Uh-oh. That bad?

She was a part-time dispatcher for the sheriff's department. While she somehow knew my date, he wasn't a sheriff. No, Mr. Chet Edwards was a stuck-on-himself city cop.

Me: Let's just say . . . no more blind dates.

Justine: Eek. Ok. Sorry.

She inserted a sad-face emoji, and I laughed. It really wasn't her fault, I suppose. She was trying to be nice. The problem was, I didn't really have the energy to date, but it didn't mean I wasn't lonely.

My phone rang, and I laughed. I knew she would be too impatient for details to keep texting.

"So how bad was it?" she demanded as soon as I answered.

"Ugh, so bad I used my mom as an excuse to leave the dinner early."

She laughed. "You're so bad."

"Seriously, why aren't there any decent guys out there? Let me clarify. Ones that are single. I swear, I'm never going to meet the right guy. Fuck my life." Not that I wanted to rush into anything, but my biological clock was ticking, and I wanted to be a mom more than anything. Maybe I'd look at a donor. It wasn't the first time I'd considered it. A man in the picture wasn't super necessary. But what a shitty thing for my kid to never have a dad. Sure, people did it all the time, but I always pictured myself finding the right guy and settling down to raise a big family.

"Maybe you're looking too hard," she mumbled around a mouthful of something.

"What are you eating?" I demanded, suddenly hungry because I'd picked at my dinner due to the self-centered A-hole ruining my appetite.

"Brownie à la mode from the diner downtown," she replied. Immediately, my mouth watered. Those things were huge and were actually meant for a couple to share.

"I'm on my way over. You better save some for me." As I slipped on my shoes and grabbed my purse, I could hear her laughing. "You're lucky you only live a block over, because any farther and I know you'd have it gone before I got there. Then we'd have big problems."

Her evil chuckle around the delectable treat spurred me on.

"Ice cream and chocolate are better than any man, anyway," she sagely informed me.

"Yeah, well they can't get you pregnant," I muttered.

"Well, depending on who brings it to you, I beg to differ."

A harumph escaped me.

"Damn that sexy stranger! He's ruined my expectations for a man. Where the hell is a man that is like him in the bedroom and just as amazing out of it?" I sighed. I was looking for a unicorn among men.

"They don't exist," she shot back with a snort. There had been a night that involved enormous amounts of wine where I'd told her my one-night-stand story. Due to the ability wine has to loosen my tongue, I hadn't held back a single detail.

"True story," I admitted with a sigh as I headed to her house to steal some of her Nirvana in a bowl.

"Your appointment is here, Hailey," the receptionist said when I answered the phone. Pinching the bridge of my nose, I closed my eyes. I'd slept like shit the night before. It might've been because I went to bed on sugar overload, but I'd deny it until my dying day. It didn't help that my dreams of the sexy stranger had left me restless, and I'd woken up gasping at least three times.

"Send him back," I huffed. Regret that I hadn't rescheduled surfaced, and my shoulders drooped. I dropped my head into my hand with a sigh.

"If this is a bad time, I can come back," a deep voice said from the doorway. Tingles of awareness skated up my spine, and a chill shot through me head to toe.

That voice.

Eyes wide, I raised my head, and my heart damn near stopped. His gaze mirrored my surprise before a wicked grin curved those perfect lips.

"You!" I gasped as my heart took off at a gallop. Inappropriate tingles started between my legs, and I knew my freaking panties were soaked.

"Well, this is a pleasant surprise," he crooned, and I wanted to swoon. Digging deep for a professionalism I wasn't feeling, I sat up straight in my chair.

"*You're* Mr. Matthews?" Well, there went my tenuous professionalism when my voice cracked.

Sexy smirk still in place, he moved all the way into my office and closed the door. His tongue wet his bottom lip. "When I told Polly to find a good replacement, I had no idea how well she'd come through."

"What? I mean, how?" I sputtered, because I couldn't seem to form a coherent thought that didn't revolve around sweeping everything from my desk, lying across it, hiking my skirt up, and begging for a repeat.

"Ms. Monroe. It is *Miss*, right?" For a split second, uncertainty flickered in his gaze.

Dumbly, I nodded.

That disarming smile was back, and my pussy gushed. If my panties weren't destroyed before, they sure as hell were after that. Obliterated. Washed away in the flood.

He took a seat in the chair opposite me. As he sprawled effortlessly and stretched his denim-clad legs out in front of him, I fought the urge to jump over my desk and into his lap.

Silently, we stared at each other, drinking in every tiny detail. At least I did. So intent was I on his head-to-toe gorgeousness, I startled slightly when he spoke.

"What do you say we take this meeting somewhere else?"
Your bed?

Aw, shit. The man was destroying the sophisticated director I'd worked so hard to maintain since getting hired at the Leon Adolescent Center three months ago. He was turning me into a puddle of lust. Literally.

"Where were you thinking?" I cautiously questioned. My damn nipples perked up at the thought of him touching them again. *Down, girls.*

"Why, Ms. Monroe, is your mind in the gutter?" he asked as his eyes dropped to my chest before slowly finding their way back up. He was reading my body and mind all too well. "I was thinking we could take this discussion to a little place I know to discuss the fundraiser over lunch. I missed breakfast, and I'm… famished."

There was no way he was unaware of the double meaning to his words. His dark blue irises glittered mischievously as his mouth twisted in humor. Narrowing my eyes, I stubbornly refused to admit he was right. Oh so very right.

Clenching my jaw, I willed the desire away to no avail. *Dammit.*

"Fine. But this is *not* a date. There will be no repeats of that night. Do not get this twisted," I weakly insisted. Despite my desperate hope for a repeat or three, I didn't want it at the potential cost of my job. Sleeping with one of the center's biggest contributors could go wrong in so many ways.

"I wouldn't dream of it," he murmured with a smirk.

My eyes traveled over his rugged frame, unwittingly admiring the way his black T-shirt stretched over his chest. Perfectly frayed jeans hugged his spread and muscled thighs. Thick black boots encased his feet. My eyes moved back up, pausing on the bulge behind his zipper. *Good God, is that his dick lying on the top of his thigh? Surely not.*

But I had firsthand knowledge of what he was packing, and I knew it was. Catching my blatant perusal, he cupped his dick and adjusted it.

Sweet baby Jesus. Heart pounding all the way down between my legs, I so wanted to do that for him.

It was then that I caught the leather vest. "Wait. You're a *biker*?"

Those midnight-blue eyes narrowed as he tensed. "Is that disdain I hear?"

"Uh, no. Not at all," I stammered. I'd had an unhealthy obsession with a certain TV biker. My one-night stand was unknowingly making himself sexier than I could've imagined.

Oh, this is bad. So damn bad.

I'd only been at my job for a few months; therefore, I was still on probation. The last thing I needed was to get caught screwing one of the benefactors of the Leon and the head of the annual fundraiser committee. But holy shit. Like I said, I remembered that night in vivid detail. Maybe I needed to review my contract—very carefully.

No! Ugh, stop!

The frown on his face dissolved, and I was once again blown away by how good-looking he was. Actually, he was damn near beautiful. My lady bits were screaming for another shot at what he could do to them.

"Well, since that's not an issue, what did you decide about lunch?" he asked as he stood.

Biting back a whimper, I made a decision that had the

potential to blow up in my face. Standing to my full height, made impressive in my heels, I almost looked him in the eye. Damn, had he been that tall last year?

He had.

Tall, muscular, sexy, captivating, and fantastic in the sack, he was every woman's wet dream. It was going to be a nearly impossible feat to keep myself from climbing his body like a damn monkey.

Okay, maybe that was a little dramatic. I did have self-control. The problem was, I didn't know if I wanted to use it. Ordinarily, I was not one to sleep around haphazardly, but that night last year had been one of vulnerability and reckless abandon.

"I'll follow you," I said with my most professional and serene smile.

Can it be to your bed, though?

Ugh.

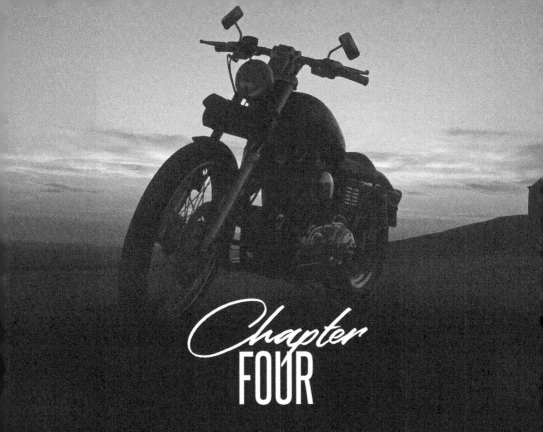

Chapter FOUR

Snow

"THE DEVIL IN I"—SLIPKNOT

THOUGH IT WAS A SHOCK, WALKING INTO THAT OFFICE TO SEE my blonde dream girl from a year ago was exactly what I needed. Especially after the shitstorm that had been brewing since then. A year later, and we were no closer to finding who was behind the distribution of Black Night.

Each time we got close, they disappeared like a fucking wraith. It was like chasing a ghost. I'd even gone so far as to reach out to my friend Decker, also known as Venom, the president of the Royal Bastards down in Ankeny. Everything they found turned out to be a dead end, telling us someone was covering their tracks well. Because if Hacker was damn good at his job, their guy Facet was better. Not that I'd ever say that to Hacker.

I backed my bike up to the curb in front of the Oasis and waited while she parked next to me. Reaper's ol' lady, Steph, stuck her head out of the door. "Hey, Snow. I knew I heard a bike. What brings you by?"

She had a fantastic menu, making the pub a great place to eat and have drinks. Since it was late afternoon, the lunch rush was over and the crowd should've dispersed. I figured it was the perfect place for me and Ms. Monroe to catch up.

"Business lunch" was all the explanation I gave her.

She appeared thoughtful as she stared at the woman parking her car, then whispered, "Okay, then. I guess I'll set up a table."

I grinned, and she giggled. She went back inside, and I turned my focus on the woman I'd secretly obsessed about for a year. The fact that she was here in my town was too mind-blowing to comprehend. Didn't mean I was going to complain.

Mesmerized, I took in every inch of her long legs as she climbed out of her vehicle. I'd forgotten how she'd fit my height perfectly. I'd barely needed to dip my head to kiss her in the heels she wore so well.

"This place is really cute! I didn't even know it was here," she exclaimed as she stopped in front of me. "Then again, I haven't had a lot of time to explore the town."

She smiled, and my insides flip-flopped. Weirdest fucking thing I'd ever experienced. I hoped I wasn't coming down with something.

"I'm glad you came, Ms. Monroe," I offered with a devilish lift of my brow. Because I really wanted her to come. All over my face.

"It's Hailey," she corrected before her pink tongue darted out to wet her lower lip. Inwardly, I groaned because I knew exactly what that tongue was capable of and I wanted to experience it again. In the worst goddamn way.

"Steph should have a table ready for us," I said as I placed a hand on her lower back and guided her into the pub. My palm burned where I touched her, wanting to explore every inch of her to see if my memory served me right.

"Steph?" she asked, with a hint of jealousy in her tone which had me smiling inside. Jealousy meant there was still interest.

"My brother's wife. She owns the Oasis." I didn't make so much as an attempt to hide my smirk. A sidelong glance at her revealed her cheeks were a rosy red. Obviously, she was aware of how she had sounded. I chuckled as we made our way to the back booth where Steph was waiting.

Once we were both seated, she placed our menus in front of us.

"You're waitressing?" I asked her with mock confusion. Truth was, I knew damn well why she was there. Her loose blonde curls were pulled up into a high ponytail, and she had her white apron on, signifying she was cooking today.

"Monica is on her break, so I'm filling in," she said with an unashamed grin. On break, my ass. Then I realized I was screwed. Because it was all fun and games until it hit me that she was going to race to the back to text or call Reaper to inform him of what she'd seen.

"Steph, this is Ms. Monroe. She's the new director at the adolescent center. We were going to meet to discuss the annual fundraiser. Figuring we could just as well discuss it over lunch,

I brought her over to check out your place because she's new to town." Damage control attempted, I waited to see if Steph would be mollified.

"Welcome to our area. Where are you from?" Steph asked, turning her attention to Hailey.

"Kansas City. And please call me Hailey," she replied with a friendly lift of her lips. Fuck, the woman was beautiful.

"Will do. Now, what can I start you off with to drink?" Steph took our drink orders and brought them back while Hailey began to peruse the menu. Steph could've saved bringing a menu for me, because I already knew what I wanted. She was sitting across the table from me.

Uh, no, I meant I knew the menu by heart.

Hell.

No, I was right the first time. It may've been a year, but I wanted Hailey Monroe. I wanted to bend her over, fist her golden hair, smack that luscious ass, and pound my cock into her tight pussy.

Those thoughts had my dick swelling painfully in my jeans. Shifting in the booth to ease some of the pressure was futile. The only thing that would provide relief was whipping my dick out of my damn pants and jerking on it. Maybe her on her knees under the table with those lips wrapped—*No!* Trying to think of the least sexy things in life didn't seem to help.

Her molten silver eyes rose to mine, her nostrils flared, and her lips parted slightly as she gazed at me. It was as if she knew every dirty thought that skipped through my brain.

"You really want to eat?" I asked in a tone husky with need.

"I actually had my lunch before you showed up," she replied, equally as labored. We stared at each other as I tried to gauge whether or not we were on the same page.

Taking a chance, I whispered, "You wanna fight, fuck, or throw rocks?"

She sucked in a sharp inhale, and lust burned in the stormy depths of her eyes.

"Decided what you want?" Steph inadvertently interrupted us when she stopped by the edge of the table.

Silence sat heavy at the table. Then Hailey swallowed hard and scooted out of the booth.

"I'm sorry, I completely forgot about a meeting I have. I need to go." She gave a brief apologetic smile to Steph and quickly headed for the door. Her heels tapped out a staccato beat on the tiled floor.

No way was she getting off that easy. Ignoring Steph's inquisitive gaze, I shot to my feet and hurried to catch up to Hailey. I caught her elbow in the entryway of the pub and spun her to face me.

"Hailey, wait!"

"Mr. Matthews, this was a mistake," she began, refusing to meet my gaze. Two rose spots colored her cheeks.

"Luke," I corrected. My hand cupping her jaw, I tipped her head up. Reluctantly, she looked at me.

"Luke." She breathed my name like a sigh.

"Why?"

"What do you mean, why? I just started my new job. I need to concentrate on that. There's no time or energy in my life for a relationship at this point. Especially not with the biggest bene-factor of the organization I work for."

She said the words, but her eyes and her pulse pounding below my little finger belied them. "Trust me when I tell you I'm not looking for a relationship."

And I wasn't. Never would, but that didn't mean that I didn't want another night with her.

"Good. Neither am I," she insisted.

Leaning forward until my lips brushed the shell of her ear, I inhaled the subtle scent of her perfume before I whispered, "Hailey? We're going to fuck—whether you want to admit it or not. Neither of us is interested in a relationship, which makes this perfect. So, let's fuck. No strings. No expectations. No rules. Well, except one. Don't develop feelings for me, because you *will* get hurt."

"What if *you* develop feelings?" she said, full of attitude that made my dick harder.

That caused me to snort laughter. "Not likely."

She appeared to consider what I'd said. Then when I thought she was gonna tell me to fuck off, she grabbed my shirt and pulled me close. Her lips hit mine, and I groaned into the kiss as my rock-hard cock pressed hard into her soft body.

Breaking apart to gasp for breath, we stared at the other. Then I demanded, "Your place or mine?"

"Which is closer?"

"I'm about five minutes from here," I growled carnally.

"I'm across town. Your place."

I nodded. "Follow me." When she told me she'd follow me from the center, I should've gone straight to my place. Cut out the bullshit in between.

She didn't argue—she simply climbed in her car, started it,

and waited expectantly. I chuckled, then climbed on my bike, pulled on my helmet, and roared down the road. A glance in my mirror showed she was still following and hadn't chickened out.

Finally, I parked in the driveway, and she pulled in next to me. Her door flew open, and those fuck-me heels clicked on the concrete as she rounded the hood. Arms crossed, she stared at me where I sat on my bike watching her.

"You gonna sit there the entire time? If so, I'm going back to work."

"Yes, ma'am," I said with a smirk and got off the bike. Like I had all the time in the world, I walked past her—enjoying her impatience.

With a glance over my shoulder, I unlocked the door. Though I wanted to shove her against it, hike up that skirt, and shove my cock so hard and deep in her cunt she saw stars, I didn't. Instead, I made my way to my room, assuming she'd follow.

Once there, I hung my cut in the closet, gripped the back of my shirt, tugged it off, and dropped it to the floor. My belt clanked as I unbuckled it and dropped my zipper. Until then, she'd watched me from the doorway.

The rasp of the zipper set her in motion. She came to stand in front of me. Slender fingers reached into my boxers and gripped my throbbing length. When her thumb swept through the bead of precum on the end and circled it around, I sucked air through my clenched teeth. No matter how unaffected I was trying to act, I lost it then.

Grasping either side of her blouse closure, I ripped it open. My actions sent buttons flying around the room. She gave a surprised squeal, and I scooped her heavy breasts out of her bra cups, then jerked her skirt up. Clasping her thighs, I hefted her against the wall to brace her and slid the crotch of her panties over to see how ready she was. She wrapped her legs around me and looped her arms around my shoulders.

"Goddamn, you're dripping wet." I groaned as I licked up the pulsing column of her slender neck, then nipped the sensitive spot below her ear. One hand cupped my head and pressed me to her as she tilted her head to the side. Her lids dropped, and she mewled as I pulled away to slip two fingers in her tight, wet slit. It only took a few skillful strokes to have my hand soaked with her excitement. Knowing she was ready, I withdrew, circled her clit, took her mouth in a punishing kiss, lined up, and slammed my cock in to the hilt.

She gasped around my tongue, and her nails dug into my shoulders. My belt was clinking with each thrust as my jeans sagged around my thighs. It was like nothing I'd experienced. Her pussy was perfect. Hot, wet, and tight. Each stroke took my breath away.

Feeling my nuts starting to pull up and my spine starting to tingle, I drove hard and deep. Her arms rested on my shoulders and held on for dear life.

"Oh God, Luke, I'm so close!" she breathlessly moaned.

Her words sent me over the edge, and I started to come. Then my eyes flew open, and I stopped.

"Shit. What the fuck are you doing to me?" I panted out before regretfully pulling out of her soaked core. No fucking condom. Goddamn it.

"Luke! Don't stop!" she gasped out.

Setting her down, I caged her against the wall as I kicked

off my pants. Her tits heaved with her labored breaths. Lowering my head to suck one in my mouth, I let it go and dropped to my knees.

Lifting one shapely thigh over my shoulder, I shoved my tongue into her pussy, reveling in her perfect tang. Like an animal, I licked and sucked with a quick nip at her pussy lip. When I rapidly circled and sucked on her clit, she came all over my face exactly how I imagined. Satisfaction bloomed in my chest as I wiped my mouth before I kissed my way up her body.

Slowly, I peeled the rest of her clothes off and then scooped her up. Reverently, I laid her on the bed. As she rested languidly on top of the comforter, I pulled a strip of condoms from the bedside drawer.

"Optimistic, aren't you?" she purred with a still-satisfied grin. Goddamn, she was hot.

"Fuck yeah, I am. You really need to get back to work?"

"No. I called Alba on the way and told her I'd be out the rest of the afternoon." Her grin turned mischievous as she rolled to her side and propped her head on her palm. Golden waves cascaded to the bed around her.

"Good." While she watched with hunger in her gaze, I rolled the first condom down my length.

"God, you're a gorgeous man." Her husky tone set my dick to jumping, and a throaty laugh escaped her.

With a growl, I crawled up between her legs, forcing her to return to her back. "Spread them wider," I demanded.

"Like this?" she murmured as she complied. Though her actions were compliant, her silvery eyes were full of mischief and fire.

"Yes," I hissed as I lined up and watched her pussy stretch around my girth. It was a beautiful sight. Once I was most of the way in, I gripped the backs of her calves and raised her long legs to give me better access.

With her thighs pushed to her chest, the angle allowed my cock to fully seat. "Holy fucking shit," I spat in a raspy voice. Even with the condom, I'd never experienced a pussy that felt better.

She chuckled, and it caused her cunt to tighten, damn near pushing me out. "Oh, hell no," I grunted as I shoved back in and began to move.

"Oh my God… yes… fuck… right there! Don't stop," she rasped out with each hard thrust. Desperate and needy, she raked her nails over my skin. I groaned as I did exactly as she instructed. I was nothing if not a dutiful pupil. The thought nearly had me laughing as I fucked her swift and hard.

It wasn't long before she was drenching my cock in her cum, pussy constricting and pulsing around me like a vise. It took supreme will not to give in to my body's desires and empty every drop in the fucking condom.

Once her spasms slowed to a flutter, I withdrew, flipped her over, and lifted her hips. With her ass in the air, I ran my palm over the smooth globes. "Have you thought about that night? Do you remember how I fucked you—what I told you?"

"Yesss," she hissed.

"Good," I replied before feeding my tip into her tight heat. Slowly, I slid inside, stroking in and out until I had worked my length all the way in. A groan escaped me as she squeezed my dick like a fist. "Jesus, this pussy is fucking amazing. Are you on birth control?"

She nodded.

"Thank fuck. We're both getting tested because I want to fuck you bare."

"Okay," she whispered.

Then I brought my fantasy to life as I wrapped her dark blonde hair in my fist and pulled her head back. The sexy curve of her neck was exposed, and I imagined marking her before she left. Back to the matter at hand, I barked out, "You wanted it hard?"

"Yes." Her reply was breathless and needy.

A wicked grin curled my lips before I smacked her ass and fucked her like my life depended on it. And it very well could.

Because she might be the death of me.

Chapter FIVE

Hailey

"GOOD DIE YOUNG"—KOE WETZEL

"I HAVE GROUND RULES," I SAID, CAUSING LUKE TO RAISE A brow. The man was sinfully hot. The slight highlights of silver in his beard were perfectly sexy. His ice-blue eyes studied me as I brushed back a dark lock of hair from his forehead.

"Okay, such as?" He rolled over and held himself propped over me. The wayward hair fell over one eye again.

"No sleepovers."

"Fine."

"No feelings."

"Trust me, I'm on board with that shit," he said with a sexy smirk that made my stomach do flip-flops. Damn, he was incredibly gorgeous.

"No one else."

"You mean like we're monogamous?"

"Yes," I firmly replied.

When he acted like he was thinking hard on that last request, I shoved at him. "Get off me! I'm not fucking sharing your dick with any random skanks. Especially if you think you'll stick it in me bare. I'll be damned. Move!" I insisted with one last shove before I realized he was laughing.

"You sure are sexy when you're pissed off," he murmured with a wicked grin that I was torn between wanting to smack off and kiss off. "Trust me, I won't need anyone else."

Bracing on his arms, he dropped down and softly brushed his lips across mine. That ended with a teasing nip before he sucked my lip in his mouth. Then he trailed kisses along my jaw, my neck, and over the swell of my breasts before tugging one nipple into his hot mouth.

A whimper fell from my lips as he licked and sucked. Nails digging into his shoulders, I shoved my head into my pillow, arched my back, and moaned. His mouth continued to work magic all over my body until I was a puddle of need.

"Please," I begged, though I had no idea what I was asking for. I simply knew I was wound tight and ready to explode. Everything he did—every touch, swipe of his tongue, and nip of his teeth drove me closer to madness.

The incredible skill with which he controlled my body should've been frightening. Instead, it was intoxicating. Each movement tore down my defenses—made me crave him.

That time he was slow, teasing, sensuous. There was no other way to explain it. He worshipped me. Maybe it was still fucking, but he sure as hell made it seem like making love. I may have lied when I told him I didn't want a relationship. Because he was the one man I would've killed to have a relationship with.

Each day for the next two weeks, I found myself anxious for the clock to hit the witching hour. Okay, so it was the end of my day, but it was definitely when the magic happened. The earliest second I could, I'd call it a day, grab my things, and meet Luke. He had quickly become a habit that I wasn't ready to kick.

Not yet.

Maybe not ever, but I wasn't sure I wanted to think about that too much right now.

My phone rang. Seeing it was Alba, I answered as I shut down my computer.

"Hey, Alba, I was just leaving." Hand in my drawer, I lifted my tote to leave.

"Hailey?" Her voice trembled, immediately drawing my undivided attention, and I froze.

"What's wrong?" The bag dropped with a thud back into my drawer. Dread pooled in my guts.

"Lynn is on the phone. Line two. It's urgent."

With a trembling hand, I hit the flashing light.

"Ms. Monroe, Danielle is gone!" Lynn shouted through the phone with a hitch in her voice.

"What?" I exclaimed, sure I had heard her wrong.

"I went to get everyone for our outing to Mel's Pizza. She wasn't in the common area. Her bed is empty, and her bag is gone."

"Lock everything down. Let's do a search of the grounds. I'll call all units and notify them we have a code silver." I hit the button I never wanted to have to touch. Code silver meant an elopement—and not the romantic kind. The kind where one of our kids ran away. Our security guard called me immediately.

"I'm on it, ma'am." I could hear he was already on the move. I shot off a brief text to Luke to let him know I had to cancel.

Everyone on staff checked every square inch of the facility and grounds. Danielle was in the least restrictive unit due to the phase she was in of her program. That meant it wasn't a gated and locked unit.

We searched the grounds, but I knew we weren't going to find her. My heart sank, and I returned to my office and called the police.

Goddamn, that was the last thing I wanted to do. Not only was I worried out of my mind for Danielle, but I was also still in my probationary period—and I lost a kid. It was so bad. So fucking bad.

"Ms. Monroe, you cannot blame yourself. These are troubled kids. This wasn't the first and likely won't be the last," Chet said as his partner stepped away to call back to dispatch. They had found footprints heading into the thickly wooded area that bordered the property and to the highway on the other side. That's where they ended.

"I understand that, but they are *my* responsibility. They are here for *help*." A shaking hand pressed to my mouth, I scanned the area again, hoping that Danielle would come walking through the trees saying she wandered off and lost track of time or something.

Of course, she didn't, and she wouldn't have packed a bag to walk in the woods. Something she also knew wasn't authorized, despite the stage she was in of treatment. We had rules, and every kid knew what was expected prior to moving up in the program.

"There will be a BOLO, uh, sorry, a 'be on the lookout' for your patient. If we hear anything, we'll let you know as soon as possible." He paused and shot a glance over his shoulder to where the other officer was still occupied and Deputy Baker was quietly observing.

"Hailey, are you sure you're okay?" he asked softly as he stepped into my personal space.

Not trusting myself with words, I nodded and stepped back.

"If you need me—" He stopped when the other cop approached. He reached into his chest pocket, then handed me his card. "If there's anything else you find or think of, please give me a call."

Holding the card, I shot him a confused glance but nodded. He knew I already had his number from our date, though I should've deleted it. Maybe he didn't want his cop friend to know we'd gone out. Too tired to worry about it, I simply stood there.

The other cop got a call and returned to their car.

"Do you want me to stop by your place to check on you?" His tone was kind—almost making me forget how self-absorbed he'd been on our date. He'd called several times since our date to ask me out again, but I'd successfully dodged setting another date.

"Um, uh, no, that won't be necessary," I stammered. "But thank you."

"Anytime, Hailey." He glanced around before he reached out and gripped my hand in an overly familiar manner.

Gently removing my hand, I crossed my arms protectively over my chest.

"I'll see you soon," he murmured, but I dismissed him.

Then they left. The sheriff's deputy finished with his questions, and he left as well. Both the sheriff's department and the city police had come in because the property for the facility was right on the edge of the city limits. The wood line was county, and since there was evidence she went into the trees, it was their investigation as well.

The night wasn't close to over for me. I had a shit ton of paperwork to do. I'd already notified all the appropriate parties, including Danielle's parents, who barely seemed concerned. That really rubbed me the wrong way.

Shoulders slumped in defeat, I returned to my office. After dropping to my chair, I began the tedious process of completing all the forms required by the facility in cases of elopement.

My phone vibrated in my purse as I was sending the last email.

A whimper escaped when I saw who it was. I set it on the desk and answered on speaker. "How did you know I needed to hear from you?"

"I didn't, but I thought you might like to stop by on your way home. I heard—" He sighed. "I mean, I really wanted to see you."

"I'll be there as soon as I lock up." My head dropped into my hands as I massaged my temples.

"See you soon," he said, then the call ended.

For a few hours, I needed to lose myself in the bearded biker that had the ability to make me forget all the bullshit. The man who was able to destroy me in the best of ways.

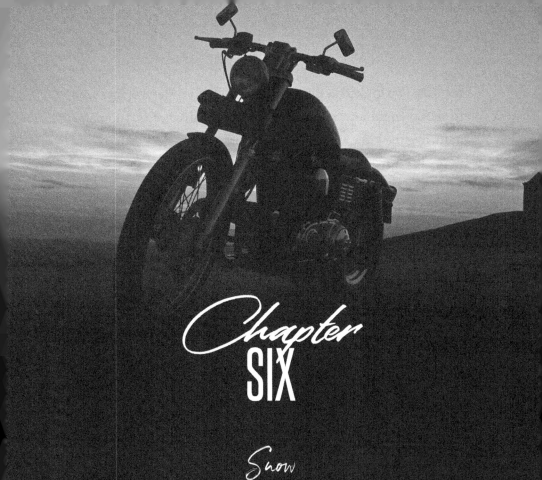

Chapter
SIX

Snow

"HUNT YOU DOWN"—SALIVA

A s I shoved my phone in my back pocket, I raked a hand through my hair. I'd nearly slipped up and given away the fact that we had access to police comms traffic. When I heard about their elopement, I had Hacker on it as soon as they'd made the call to law enforcement.

Once I got home, I planned to talk to Baker to see what he'd heard. Though the facility itself wasn't county, the Leon was on the edge of town and bordered the city limits. They had been called in because Danielle had gone through the trees into county territory.

"Still nothing. I've searched every camera in town that

records. I've looked at everything from before she was last seen to about ten minutes ago. I checked buses, cabs, hotels, you name it. It's like the kid vanished into thin air." Hacker ran a tatted hand down his face before he fell back in his chair.

"Thanks, brother. I appreciate you staying late for this. Now get out of here. I'm sure Kassi and the kids are waiting on you."

"I have some programs running that will notify me if she pops up anywhere in the area through facial recognition." He stood from his desk with the multiple monitors. I nodded.

"Sounds good. I'm gonna have the guys keep their eyes peeled. Will you be in tomorrow morning? I wanna have a brief church to discuss this."

He nodded. "Yeah, but only for a few hours. Sebastian has a doctor's appointment that I want to be there for."

His oldest kid had been a preemie, and they monitored his development closely. He was a pretty awesome and wild little kid. One who made it easy to forget he'd been touch and go for the first several months of his life.

"Roger that. Well, I'm out too."

We walked to the bikes, and as I reached for my helmet, Soap, Reaper, Hollywood, and Blue walked out of the shop next door. Leaving the brain bucket hanging on the handle, I waited until they got to the bikes.

"Hey, Prez. You heard about the kid at the Leon?" Reaper asked with a furrowed brow.

"Yeah, I've had Hacker looking into it. I was gonna send out a message for you all to be watchful and to call church for tomorrow. Truthfully, I wanted to have us get on our bikes and scour town, but I don't think that will get us anywhere. There's the chance she may have simply run off, and if she did, she's long gone," I muttered.

"I don't like it," said Hollywood, devoid of his usual grin. Soap stood next to his bike but made no move to leave.

"Trust me, neither do I," I said before pulling my helmet over my head and securing the strap. I lifted my bike from the kickstand and flipped it up. The center was successful, and kids rarely ran off—maybe one every few years. Yet this was the fourth one this year, and none of them had been found. Polly had been beside herself before she left. Restless energy surged through me. "You staying here tonight, Soap?"

"Yeah. Blue and I are gonna have a few beers and shoot some pool," he said as he dropped his gaze to the ground, and he gripped the back of his neck. I knew why he wanted to stay; I wasn't stupid. But I hoped he knew what the fuck he was doing.

"What time tomorrow?" Reaper asked as he swung a leg over his seat.

"Bright and early. Zero seven. Hacker has somewhere to be, so I want to be done in time for him to go." Everyone nodded or gave a chin lift.

"Hey, Prez. Steph wanted me to invite you for dinner. I almost forgot with all this crap." Reaper slid his shades on and looked in my direction.

"Think I'm just gonna head home." There was something I needed more than food. Though Steph's cooking was to die for, it wouldn't satisfy the craving I had. "Tell her I said thanks." With that, I started my engine, revved the throttle, and pulled out. The roar of bikes followed me as Reaper pulled alongside and the others fell in behind.

One by one, we split off in different directions.

By the time I got to my house, I needed to burn off some restless energy something fierce. I was relieved to see my porch light on. A tired grin lifted the corner of my mouth when I saw that light.

Hailey had a remote to my garage so she could park her car in there when she was here. She wanted to believe no one would know she was coming over. I snorted as I parked in my driveway. She obviously didn't know how small towns worked.

Deciding I could talk to Baker in the morning, I sent him a text, then got off my bike and headed up my walk.

When I went inside, I smelled something delicious. The scent led me to the kitchen.

"Did you cook?" I asked as she was carrying two plates to the table.

A huff of dry laughter escaped her. "Not hardly. I stopped and grabbed Chinese."

"Good enough for me," I said as I approached her when she set the food down.

My hand curled around her neck, and I gave her what was supposed to be a brief kiss. Except, it had been a shit day for us both, and she gripped my shirt tightly. Lost in her taste, I drove my fingers into her tangled waves.

Finally out of breath, we broke apart. Gripping her hair in my hands, I rested my forehead on hers.

"We need to hurry up and eat," she gasped through kiss-swollen lips. My beard had left her chin slightly red, and I ran a thumb over the lightly abraded skin.

"We can eat after," I offered.

"No, because I won't want to leave the bed for a while, and I'm going to need my energy," she replied with a wry quirk of her mouth.

"I like the way you think." I grinned, sitting at the table.

We went over the day's events, but she wasn't telling me much I didn't already know. She pushed the rest of her food around on her plate for a bit, then dropped her fork and slid the dish away.

"Hey, why don't we go lie down? I'll just hold you. I'm not worried about fucking tonight." I was startled at my offer. This, what we had, was *only* supposed to be about fucking. Not dinner, not cuddling—none of that shit. Not sure how to process everything, I decided to let it simmer for a while, and I'd analyze it later.

We left the plates on the table, and she quietly led the way to my room. I watched her ass sway as she moved down the hall.

When she stopped by the bed, I wordlessly helped her undress and held the covers up for her to climb in. I stripped to my boxer briefs and scooted her to the center of the bed before getting in behind her.

She only lay with her back to my front for a handful of moments before she rolled to face me. Her kiss was featherlight, followed by the tip of her tongue teasing between my lips.

"I need you to work your magic. Make nothing matter but how hard you make me come." It was a demand and a plea all in one. The pain in her eyes cut me to the quick.

"You sure?"

At her nod, I shucked my drawers and buried my hand in the golden tresses at the base of her skull before I slipped a leg between hers. My erection twitched in expectation and slipped in the precum that immediately painted her abdomen.

Slowly, I kissed and ran my tongue down the side of her neck, pausing over the pulse that pounded there. There was something about the taste of her skin that drove me wild. Teasingly, I took my time—savoring every inch of her until I couldn't handle it anymore and I needed to consume her.

"Luke," she said on a breathy exhale when my mouth found her wet pussy. When I pulled back and slipped one finger, then two, and curled them, she clutched my hair and moaned. That wasn't good enough, though. I wanted to hear her scream.

In all the best ways.

Everything about her hit my senses until my nerve endings were in overdrive. I wanted to drive into her, but I needed to taste her on my tongue first. To hold her in place, I slipped my free arm under her thigh to place a flat palm over her abdomen. A sharp inhalation preceded her grip tightening on my hair, which told me she was close. Relentless, I flicked her clit with the tip of my tongue, then alternated circling and sucking.

Satisfaction hit me when she arched her back, ripped at my hair, and screamed my name over and over until her grip loosened and her screams trailed off. Her chest heaved, and she kept whispering "Oh my God."

As she whispered, I moved up her body, spreading her legs with my hips. A few shallow strokes and I was fully seated. Sharply, I sucked air in through my teeth. She wrapped her legs around me, and her sheath tightened around my cock. It had my heart slamming against my rib cage.

Something shifted as I held my weight off her and stared into her eyes. Not that I could put my finger on it, but the awe in her eyes matched with the soft parting of her kiss-swollen lips made me feel like the king of the world.

"Fuck, you're so tight and so wet," I said through my groan. I wanted to flip her around and drive into her from behind, but it seemed like she needed it slow tonight.

"Luke, fuck me hard," she pleaded, and I sucked in a startled breath.

I was wrong.

"Are you sure?" I asked as my traitorous cock wept with glee.

"I'm sure. I need this," she murmured. "I need you."

I withdrew slowly, then slammed home, and she gasped. Her hands left my shoulders to grip the headboard, and I immediately missed them.

Listening to the steady slap of our skin, I stared into her eyes. Her tits bounced with each thrust, and I adjusted my weight to one arm so I could tweak her nipples one at a time. The way she tightened around me as I did it, told me she loved every minute.

"I don't know how much longer I can hold off," I warned as I kept my pace.

"I'm almost there" was her gasping response. Barely four strokes in and her walls tightened around my cock, then pulsed with her powerful orgasm. Unable to hold back, I withdrew, stroked my length, and came all over her soft abdomen.

"Holy shit," I breathlessly cried as I released my dick.

"You can say that again."

For the next two hours, the only important things in my world were the bliss I saw on her face with each orgasm and the ecstasy I found in her body.

By the time we were a sweaty tangle of exhausted limbs, I'd

blown through three condoms. I vowed those would be the last I used.

After dumping the latest one in the bathroom trash, I came back to find her sprawled facedown with the sheet riding low on her hips. She was beautiful in repose. The lines of her back sloped flawlessly into the perfect curve of her ass. My brain wanted to pick apart my thoughts from earlier, but I refused.

Telling myself I was only going to hold her for a bit before I woke her up to go home, I wrapped myself around her soft, perfect body. And promptly fell asleep.

The ringing of my phone woke me. Disoriented, I looked around in confusion before I leaned over and fumbled around with my jeans to get to the back pocket. The time said it was barely five in the morning.

"Yeah," I said in a voice hoarse from sleep.

"Prez, I got bad news." Hacker's voice was low and unsteady.

That woke me up in a hurry, and I sat up. My eyes locked on Hailey's naked body curled up in my bed. *Shit*.

"Should we call everyone in now?" I asked as I prepared to get out of bed.

"Vinny will send the message out now with your approval," he responded.

"Do it. I'll be there in fifteen." Tossing the phone to the nightstand, I gently shook her shoulder.

"Babe, we fell asleep. It's five o'clock." The words had no sooner left my lips than she bolted up with her locks a wild mess.

"In the morning?" she shouted as she shoved the curtain of

her hair out of her face, eyes wide in unhappy surprise. Tits bared to my view, nipples peaked from the AC, she whipped the covers back. I fought a groan as my cock came to life.

"Yeah," I said as I cupped one tit and hefted it in my hand. My fingertips teased her nipple. More than anything, I wanted to lean over and pull that peak into my mouth, but the realistic side of me surfaced. "I need to go into the clubhouse. Something came up."

She was already out of the bed and pulling her clothes on. The entire time, she was muttering about fucking up, that she should've been home hours ago, that she hoped no one else was awake.

If I didn't have a situation to tend to, I might've found it funny and pulled her back into bed. Since I did, I chuckled at her and shook my head. When I walked my naked ass toward the bathroom to grab a quick shower, she darted out of the room.

"Later!" she yelled down the hall before I heard the kitchen door close and then the garage door rolling up.

Shaking my head again, I rushed through cleaning the smell of sex off me, getting dressed, and out the door.

That turned out to be a day I wished I'd said fuck it and stayed in bed.

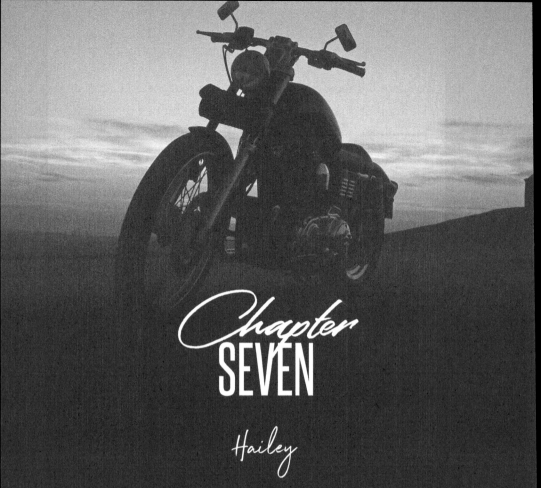

Chapter
SEVEN

Hailey

"COME A LITTLE CLOSER"—CAGE THE ELEPHANT

A ll day, I'd hoped that we'd hear something good about Danielle's whereabouts. Yet as I prepared to leave for the day, there still hadn't been a word.

I shot a text to Luke to see if he wanted to come to my place tonight. My tub was bigger than his, and I wanted to soak before he came over.

Luke: Can't tonight. Club stuff.

"Well, that sucks," I muttered.

My heart dropped as I read the words, and I realized I was way more disappointed that my casual-sex partner was bailing on me than I should be. Except I wasn't ready to think about that. Unfortunately, a little voice in the back of my head called me a liar and insisted my emotions were already tangled.

"Um, are you okay?" I looked up to see Justine standing in my doorway, obviously listening to me talk to myself.

"Hey, girl," I said with a tired smile. "Sorry, just thinking out loud."

"I thought maybe after yesterday you could use a drink. Now I see I was right. We can either hit the Oasis, or I have a few bottles of wine chilling at my place."

As a dispatcher, she knew what had happened.

The thought of going to the Oasis made me think of Luke again. Bad idea.

"Let's go to your place."

"Sounds good. Then if we drink too much, I can stumble to bed and you can crawl on the couch." She chuckled, and with drooping shoulders, I grabbed my shit and followed her outside.

"I'm going to stop by my house to grab a change of clothes. You know, just in case," I said with a heavy sigh, though I had no intention of getting blitzed on wine.

"Babe, don't worry about it. You can fit in my clothes."

"Okay, but I draw the line at wearing your panties. I'm washing mine." I wrinkled my nose, and she laughed.

"Whatever trips your trigger. Let's go. Wine awaits."

I followed her to her place and parked on the street. She had a single-lane driveway and a small garage full of the things she'd gotten when her mom passed away. Her place was little but tidy.

She was unlocking her side door as I climbed out of my car. Shouldering my bag, I traipsed up to follow her inside. When she flipped on the lights, I dropped my stuff on her counter.

"Let me grab you some comfy clothes," she said and disappeared into her room. She returned to toss me some unicorn leggings and an oversized T-shirt that said, "I got lucky at the Shamrock." There was the silhouette of a pole dancer. I shook my head with a huffed laugh.

"Where the hell did you get this?" I asked as I held up the shirt.

A secretive smirk was followed by "Go change and I'll tell you."

"Uh-huh. Is it clean, and was it Phillip's?" Phillip was her ex-boyfriend who had cheated on her with one of the strippers from that place named Cherry. She was a skanky bitch.

She laughed as she comically waggled her brows. "Definitely not Phillip's."

Wanting to know the story, I hurried to the bathroom to change, and she went into her room still laughing. Once we were both sitting in her living room, candles burning and wineglasses filled, I demanded, "Okay, spill."

With a half shrug followed by a dreamy look, she said, "I had a one-night stand with a bad boy."

"Good for you," I said, raising my glass in salute. "So how was it?"

"Amazing and all damn night. Unfortunately, not long-term material. Now that I've told you my secret… what's the deal with you and Snow?"

"Snow?" I asked as if I was confused.

"Girl, do not play dumb with me. Luke Matthews. President of the Demented Sons, all-around Hottie McSizzle, and quick on his way to being the town's sexiest silver fox." Her lips curled in self-satisfaction as she took a sip of the deep red wine.

"I'm not sure what you mean," I offered before I gulped my entire glass and poured another. When I looked up, she was leaning forward, elbows on her knees and glass dangling by the brim from her fingertips.

Dammit, I had hoped to tell Justine before she found out from gossip.

"Hailey. This is small-town Iowa. There are no secrets in a place like this." Her deadpan expression accompanied her long, measured stare and another sip of wine.

My breath came in short spurts, and sweat broke out over my lip. No one was supposed to know. Then again, when I left his house that morning, I was observed by Luke's nosey neighbor outside with her dogs. At five in the morning. Who was up that early? Other than nosey neighbors, I guess.

"Who told you?"

"Edith Bowman," she said with pursed lips.

"Oh my God! She just saw me this morning!" Edith was Luke's neighbor. She was also Alba's mother. I hadn't known that before today when she'd "popped in" to see if Alba wanted to go to lunch. The woman had to be eighty-five if she was a day, but as spry and sharp as someone half her age. And obviously more than nosey; she was a gossip.

"Well, after her lunch with her daughter, she stopped by

the station to make a noise complaint. Seems her neighbor rides a loud motorcycle and often gets home late at night." Justine smirked. I sighed and rolled my eyes.

"Jesus deliver me from old busybodies and relentless friends," I muttered before I guzzled my glass dry again. The last of the bottle filled it up.

"So, are you seeing him then?" she prodded. An excited gleam was in her eye as she leaned forward. Honestly, I was waiting for her to clap her hands and bounce in her seat.

"No. It's just, um, well… we both lead busy lives, and neither of us has time or energy for a relationship."

"But you have the energy for hot wild monkey sex?"

"Oh, for the love of God, Justine."

"Is he good? Please tell me he's good. No. Scratch that. Tell me he's a fucking machine. Tell me you have countless orgasms at the mercy of his massive dick! Is he hung?" At her words, my face heated.

"I—" My mouth flopped open and closed like a fish as I tried to decide how to answer that. I'd never been one to kiss and tell.

"He is! Holy shit! You better give me the deets. Right. Effing. Now! My bad boy was several months ago. I need to live vicariously through you!" she whined and held her hands as if in prayer—with a wineglass in them.

"I'm not discussing my sex life!" If I thought my cheeks couldn't burn hotter, I was so wrong. I was pretty sure there were flames licking at them.

"Then at least tell me—more than one orgasm a night?"

I pulled my lips between my teeth and nodded. She squealed excitedly.

"Every night?" Her eyes twinkled, and glee curled her lips.

"Most," I finally admitted.

"Well, hot damn, that's what I'm talking about!"

I was surprised she was insanely ecstatic for me. "Really?"

"Girl, fuck the gossipmongers and bang Luke 'Snow' Matthews as long and as hard as you can." I about choked on my tongue when she said it like that.

Instead, I finished the wine and opened the second bottle.

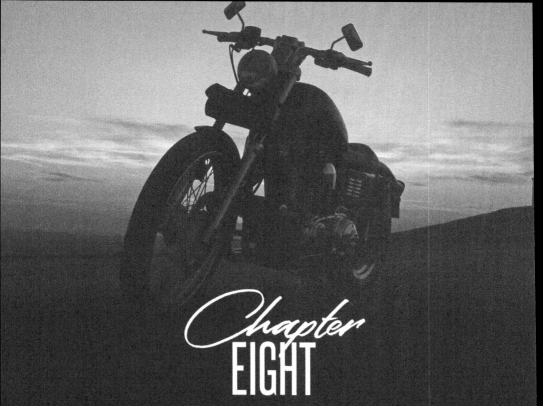

Chapter EIGHT

Snow

"BAD COMPANY"—FIVE FINGER DEATH PUNCH

"YOU FOUND A TICKET THAT WAS PURCHASED IN DANIELLE'S name, but she never got on any of the buses?" I asked Hacker as he sat at the table looking pissed. He hated it when he couldn't find something.

"Yeah. I'm telling you; I watched every second of video from the bus station. She wasn't there." He crossed his arms.

"Do you know who bought the ticket?" Soap asked.

"That's another weird thing. It was bought online after I'd checked everything the night it happened. Whoever paid for it used a VPN and paid with a bogus digital account funded by multiple deposits from various other digital accounts. None secured with an actual bank account. I've never reached so many dead ends in a search. It was intentional, and someone was seriously covering their tracks," Hacker muttered with a deep frown.

"So it was an attempt to lead authorities away from here to make it look like Danielle left the area to go home to Phoenix," Reaper mused as he tapped the table.

"That's what I was thinking," I said with a frustrated sigh.

We hashed out everything we knew—which wasn't much.

Other than making sure everyone was updated on what had happened with Danielle and finding out someone bought a bullshit ticket, church hadn't been overly productive.

It hadn't given us any information we didn't already have, and I'd regretted cutting my morning short with Hailey. Not that I could've made her stay, but it would've been fun trying to convince her. Nor did we have any leads on the supplier of Black Night.

It seemed like we ended the meeting with more questions than we started with. After everyone dispersed and got to work, I returned a call to Baker. I told him what Hacker found out about the ticket. Neither they nor the city cops had found that yet. He told me he didn't have anything to add but would touch base with me later, then hung up.

"Goddamn it," I cursed as I tossed my phone to my desk.

Figuring I might as well head over to the Shamrock a little early, I hopped on my bike and drove to Spirit Lake. It was summer, and with all the college kids and the tourists at the lakes, we were hopping. Then again, without much to do in our area besides ice fishing and snowmobiling, the Shamrock was a busy place in the winter too.

Zena was my manager there, and she was able to handle most things pretty well. At one time, she'd been one of our dancers. Until she reached an age where she thought she was too old to be on stage. I'd always liked her, and she had a good head on her shoulders. That's why it had been a no-brainer when old Tom retired to Florida and I needed a new manager.

She knew the girls, knew what to look for in new dancers, knew the Shamrock like the back of her hand, ran a tight ship, and had been there over ten years. With her in charge, the Shamrock was in good hands. Business was better than good.

"Hey, gorgeous," she called out as I let myself in the back door. She lit a cigarette and inhaled deeply before blowing a cloud above her head. I raised my brow at her bold audacity.

"Zena, you know there's no smoking in here since they passed that ordinance."

She smirked. "So fire me."

I laughed. We had the same conversation every time I came over.

"Why are you here, anyway?" she asked as she took another drag.

"I figured I'd sign the checks. I'm a little early, but I'll take the deposit to the bank too," I said. She nodded, and I followed her back to the office to sit at the desk.

That one day a week I signed the checks was also the day I collected the cash from the extracurricular activities that didn't run through the bar's till. They were a large source of income.

After signing everything, I stood.

She opened the safe, handed me the bank deposit, then rolled the chair to the side. I lifted the plastic chair mat and rolled the rug up. The second safe was in the floor under all that shit.

As I pulled the stacks of cash out, I raised a brow. "Damn. Busy week?"

A bark of laughter escaped her. "Yeah, you could say that. Gina's pretty popular. We get a lot of requests for her *private dances.*"

"I'd say." We weren't pimps, but if the girls wanted to make extra money during their private dances, they paid a portion of what they made. It covered the use of the safe space the strip club afforded and us turning a blind eye to their extracurricular activities. There were rarely issues, because one or more of us were often there to help keep things in line. We had good bouncers, trained by Bull, who held shit together when we weren't around.

The cops looked the other way because half of them were customers. They couldn't take us down without implicating half the force in the process.

"Wendy wanted to know if she could get an occasional customer in the private rooms."

My gaze locked on her. "You trust her?"

She gave me an eye roll that I wouldn't have tolerated from many. "Please. Do you think I'd have her working for me if I thought she wasn't trustworthy?"

"True. Then do what you see fit. Ensure she knows the cut."

"Will do." Her knowing eyes trailed over me. "Something different about you."

"Huh?" I blurted out as I tucked the cash into the inner pockets of my cut.

"You look… different. Can't put my finger on it, though." She tapped a bloodred nail to her lip.

"I got a haircut?" I offered.

"No. Not like that. It's something in your eyes."

"More wrinkles?" I joked. She glared.

"Boy, you're the same age as me, so if you start saying you're old, I'm gonna kick your ass." I laughed at her exaggerated snarl. She'd had a bit of a rough life, so she definitely didn't sport a youthful glow, but other than smoking, she took care of herself.

"Boy? If we're the same age, which I know we are, how are you gonna call me boy?" I tried to hide my grin. Zena was fun to spar with, but we'd never taken it further than that. She'd offered in the past, but I'd been with Cammie. Zena had never offered again. Not even after Cammie left.

"Well, I figure if I can convince you that you're a boy, then it means I'm young too!" She chortled at her humor. Though I wanted to roll my eyes, her laughter was infectious.

"I gotta go, babe. Anything else you need from me?"

"Yeah, the blue room needs new speakers. Two of them are all crackly."

"I'll have Soap come over to check on it."

"Mmm, maybe someone else. Unless you have him come early. Like way early." I gave her a curious glance, and my eyes narrowed.

"Why? He do something I should know about?" At my question, she looked slightly uncomfortable. She wouldn't meet my gaze, and she shifted from foot to foot.

"He kinda lost his shit the other night."

"Kinda?" I crossed my arms and raised a brow as I waited for her to elaborate.

"Yeah. Tash was dancing, and some dude got handsy. Bull would've handled it, but he didn't get a chance. Soap was all over the dude—hauled him outside and would've beat the dog shit out of him if Bo wasn't coming in from his break and stopped him." She looked worried.

"Had he been drinking?" I already knew the answer, but I needed verification. She closed her eyes and sighed.

"He always does. First drink starts the minute Tash takes the stage, and he doesn't quit."

"Goddamn it. I'll deal with him," I promised before I grabbed the bank bag.

"What I don't understand is why he doesn't just claim her and get her ass outta here," Zena said.

It was my turn to sigh. "I don't know," I lied. It wasn't my story to tell.

We said our goodbyes, and I left for the bank.

After that, I went to the clubhouse. When I pulled into the lot, I frowned. There was a cruiser parked in front of the doors. Of course.

Not wasting time, I got off my bike and tugged off my helmet. I hung it on the handlebar, finger-combed my hair back, and stood.

Stepping into the dim, cool interior, I saw the broad back of a sheriff's deputy talking to Vinny and Hacker.

"Is there a problem?" I asked. Baker turned to face me, and I saw the lines between his brows.

"You got a minute?" he asked in his deep baritone.

"Yeah, let's go in my office." Baker nodded, and they all followed me down the hall.

"You on the clock or off?" It was my way of asking if this was an official or unofficial visit.

"Off."

I nodded.

"They found the girl from the Leon." His eyes went back and forth as he looked from one of my eyes to the other. I didn't like the fact that he didn't say they found her safe.

Baker was a tough bastard. I'd known him all my life. The way his face was ashen and the lines framed the edge of his mouth wasn't a common look for him. The fact that he palmed his jaw and scrubbed over his mouth was disconcerting as well.

"You gonna tell me the details?" I asked, tired of waiting. Knowing it was bad, I grabbed the shot glasses and whiskey from my drawer. While I waited for his response, I poured us each a shot.

Keeping one for myself, I slid the rest across the desk.

Baker's shoulders slumped a bit, and he reached for a small glass. Vinny and Hacker grabbed one too.

Without a word, we each downed the rich amber liquid and slammed the glass to the desktop. Baker's green eyes met mine.

"It was bad, brother," he croaked out.

He proceeded to tell us she was found in Fort Defiance Park by some hikers. She appeared to have been raped, assaulted, and asphyxiated. Preliminary autopsy would be done in the Iowa state medical examiner's office down in Ankeny to confirm. The evidence had all been collected and sent to the Iowa Division of Criminal Investigations for examination.

"Jesus," Vinny said as he leaned against the wall. My gaze locked on Hacker's, and he gave a slight raise of his chin.

"I'm out, unless you still need me," he said. I motioned that he was free to go. Vinny glanced at Hacker as he exited the office. We both knew he'd be going straight to his computers to start creeping into their database.

"How the hell is this shit happening here?" Baker asked, looking sick to his stomach. It was a feeling I shared with him. Danielle was just a kid.

"I have no idea, but I'm going to do my best to find out," I promised. He nodded, then took a deep breath.

"I'm out too," he finally said. "And as always, you didn't hear any of that from me. They won't be publicly announcing it yet."

"Bro, I got you." We had a long-standing and good working relationship with the sheriff's department. They appreciated the shit we did to keep the county safe and tended to look the other way if our methods got a little on the wrong side of the law. As long as innocent people didn't get hurt, that was.

The local cops, however, were an entirely different story. They had a hard-on for us a mile long. If they could fuck us, they were gonna do it.

Baker left, and I went to Hacker.

"Find anything?"

He looked haggard and drawn as his eyes lifted from the screen.

"According to the preliminary reports the sheriff's department filed, none of her belongings were with her."

"With her being found outside of town in an area that was

searched, she couldn't have been far from the area while she was missing. We need to figure out where she was."

"And fast."

On my way home, I stopped by Hailey's place, but it was dark, and she wasn't home. Though I'd told her I couldn't stop by, I changed my mind. It was late, but I was hoping to let off some steam with her, so it left me feeling disgruntled that she wasn't there.

I really didn't like that feeling. It shouldn't drive me crazy that she wasn't home and I didn't know where she was. I shouldn't need her to the level of desperation.

A handful of times in her pussy and I was an addict—her, my drug of choice.

Fucking hell.

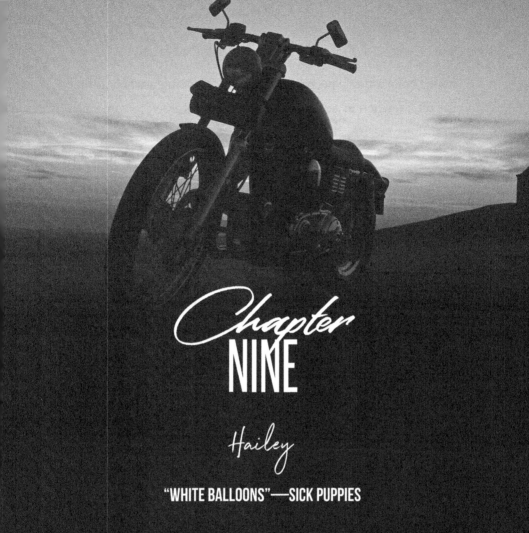

Chapter
NINE

Hailey

"WHITE BALLOONS"—SICK PUPPIES

I'D BEEN KICKING MYSELF ALL DAY FOR MY POOR DECISIONS THE night before. My pounding head wouldn't quit, I'd puked up the lunch Justine had packed for me, and my eyes were burning. Wine hangovers were the worst for me, which was why I usually only had a few glasses max, not a few *bottles*.

There had been no word on Danielle. I'd called the police station to see if they'd heard anything, but of course, they had nothing to report on an ongoing investigation. I'd barely gotten a thing done.

The day had been so awful, I hadn't had time to realize there hadn't been a single peep from Luke since last night when he blew me off. So when he sent me a text to see if I wanted to come over, I sat there staring at my phone.

The thought of doing anything but curling up in a ball made me start dry heaving.

Me: Tonight's not a good night.

The dots flashed, then disappeared several times. My brow lowered in confusion. It made me wonder what the heck he was typing and erasing.

Except the message that came through was one word.

Luke: Fine.

"Fine? That's it? Fine?" I asked out loud, flabbergasted. It kind of hurt my feelings that he didn't push a little harder than that. Despite it being me who said it wasn't a good night.

Then I laid my forehead to the cool wood of the desk. It was time to call it a day. I was being irrational, and I needed my bed. My hand fumbled blindly for the phone. When I bumped the receiver, it fell to the desktop with a clatter that made me wince. Then I felt around until I hit the first button on the bottom row.

"Yes, Hailey?" Alba asked entirely too cheerfully, in my opinion.

"I'm not feeling well. I think I'm going to leave a little early."

"Is there anything I can do?" she asked kindly.

"No, but thank you."

I ended the call and pulled my drawer open with my head still on the desk. The sunglasses I'd borrowed from Justine as she'd laughed in my face that morning went back on.

"Good night," Alba called out, and I gave a silent wave without glancing her way.

My feet were killing me as I crossed the lot and got in my car. Justine's shoes were a size too small, but they matched the blouse I'd borrowed from her perfectly.

I'd gone straight home. The drive was made in blessed silence. After I parked in the garage, drew all the blinds, pulled all the drapes, and kicked off my shoes, I popped a couple of Tylenol. Then I shuffled to my room, dropped my clothes to the floor, and fell into bed. Except, no matter how hard I tried, I couldn't fall asleep. It was all I wanted—well, that and my head to quit hammering.

"God, if you make my head quit pounding, I'll never drink cheap wine again," I muttered from under my pillow.

Finally unable to stand it anymore, I got up and took one of the sleeping pills I had in case of insomnia. I hated them because the dreams were horrendously vivid and the occasional sleepwalking wasn't great either. Once, I'd gotten up and started cooking macaroni and cheese.

Seriously, I'd woken up the next day to find the orange cheese powder all over my hands, pajamas, and bedding. The mess from my attempt was scattered on the stove and floor. I didn't remember doing any of it. That was the last time I'd taken one, but I was desperate to sleep and get this headache to stop.

Downing a full bottle of water, I shuffled back to bed.

Darkness had descended and I was starting to feel sleepy when I thought I heard a motorcycle draw near. It seemed to idle outside my house, but then took off. Disappointment spread through my chest, because it would've been nice to have Luke hold me like he had the other night.

My eyes grew heavy, and I was out.

My dreams were plagued by a bearded biker who kissed me from head to toe before making me scream his name.

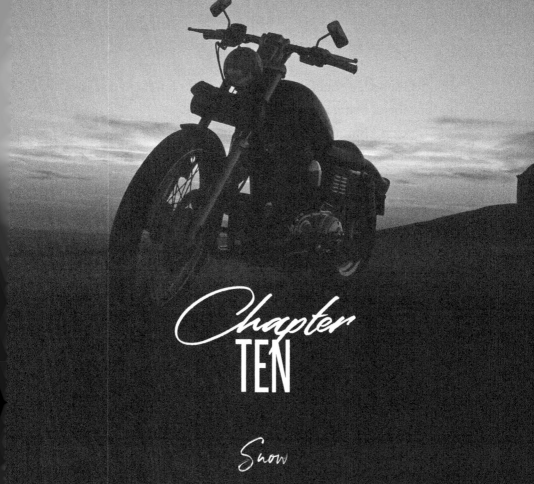

Chapter
TEN

Snow

"LOCKED & LOADED"—GODSMACK

HAD TEXTED HER TO SEE IF SHE WANTED TO HOOK UP. WHEN she told me it wasn't a good night, I started to tell her I could be there for her. Hell, I'd started to offer to pick her up some of the ice cream she had said was her favorite.

Instead, I erased every word that made me sound like a pussy-whipped idiot and replied with "Fine."

Still, after I left the clubhouse, I proceeded to stop into Fareway and grab a pint of that disgustingly sweet shit anyway.

Except when I arrived at her house, there wasn't a light on in the place, all the blinds were drawn, and I didn't see her car.

Again. Granted, it could've been in the garage, but the house gave off the vibe of being silent and empty.

"Fuck it," I muttered and headed home.

Entering the kitchen through my garage, I tossed my keys on the counter and dropped the melting ice cream in the trash.

Walking past the framed picture of me and my brother, I paused. It had been taken when I was in high school, right before graduation. For a few minutes, I did my best to deal with the pain that never really went away.

With a heavy sigh, I went to take a hot shower. All night as I tossed and turned, I wondered who Hailey had been with the last two nights. It could've been a friend, but maybe it wasn't. What if it hadn't been a friend? What would I do about it if that was the case?

We said no one else.

Perhaps she was done with me.

Well, fuck it. It was good while it lasted, because if she was with someone else, I was the one that was done.

Chapter
ELEVEN

Hailey

"THE LONG DEFEAT"—THRICE

THE NEXT MORNING, I WAS A NEW WOMAN. THERE WERE NO signs that I'd gotten up and done anything weird, and I didn't remember dreaming anything crazy. Thank the good Lord above.

Dressed in a sleeveless gray dress, I topped it with a summer-weight sweater. Once I swiped a layer of gloss on my lips and a little mascara on my lashes, I called it good.

Luke could kiss my ass since he didn't seem to have time for me. Feeling confident in my decision, I drove to work bright and early. Alba wasn't in yet, so I dropped the mail on her counter and headed back to my office.

With a sigh, I dumped my purse on the desk, shed the sweater to the back of my chair, and moved to the window. Pulling back the curtains and opening the blinds, I stared outside deep in thought, worried about Danielle.

"Hailey."

I jumped and screeched in surprise as I spun to the door. My hand splayed over my heart as I fought to slow its pace and catch my breath. "Jesus, Luke! You scared the shit out of me!"

He at least looked chagrined. "Sorry, I thought you heard me come in. You really shouldn't leave the door unlocked when you're here alone."

"Well, then I guess it's a good thing you're here. Now I'm not alone," I snarked.

Hands shoved deep in his dark, tattered jeans, he chewed on the inside of his cheek nervously. My gaze narrowed on him as I tried to figure out what was going on. The man didn't do nervous. He was the most confident and assured man I'd ever met.

"Why are you here so early? Especially after not having anything to do with me for the last two nights?" I'd told myself I wasn't going to bring it up because we weren't in a relationship, but my word vomit overrode my clouded brain.

"What the hell are you talking about?" he barked as he took a step toward me. The closer he came to my airspace, the less control I had over my body and mind. I took a self-preserving step back.

"You blew me off the other night, then I didn't hear a word from you last night either." I inwardly winced, knowing I'd been the one to tell him it wasn't a good night. My damn mouth refused to stay shut. No matter how hard I tried, I couldn't help coming off as a bitchy girlfriend, which I definitely was not. Unfortunately, he'd created an addiction within me worse than any drug.

I'd become addicted to *him*. His scent, his eyes, the boyish flop of hair that refused to behave, the sound of his voice, and that body—good God, that body. Every bit of him was a potent aphrodisiac that left me intoxicated and wanting.

Two steps farther and he was in front of me, toe to toe. Heart fluttering wildly, I moved again, but my back hit the wall. He leaned forward, eyes locked on mine, and trailed his fingertips up the bare skin of my arm. A shiver shot through me.

His dark blue gaze dropped to where my nipples were embarrassingly screaming for his attention. Those perfect lips twitched slightly at one corner before he ran his fingertips over the peaks on my chest. I gasped as I fought the need to shamelessly shove them into his hand.

"You think I blew you off?" he whispered seductively as he leaned forward to run the tip of his nose along the shell of my ear. He inhaled me deeply before exhaling across my neck. Rough skin lightly snagged along the soft knit fabric of my dress as he moved up to wrap his hand lightly around the front of my throat.

Words escaped me as my breaths came in rapid succession. The pressure of his grip increased only slightly as his thumb stroked under my jaw.

"Cat got your tongue, Hailey?" His mouth teased featherlight kisses along my jaw before he nipped my ear. "I think it was you who was evading me. You didn't come home for the last two nights. Where were you, Hailey? Who were you with? And tell me—does it feel like I was blowing you off?" He pressed his erection into my hip as he whispered in my ear. My eyes fell shut as my lips parted wantonly.

A throat clearing made my eyes pop open and dart toward the sound. Officer Edwards stood in the doorway, face impassive and eyes cold. "I'm sorry to interrupt," he said, and I thought I detected a slip in his calm demeanor. "But I need to speak with you, Ms. Monroe."

Luke's head slowly swiveled toward the police officer in the doorway, his nose skimming the surface of my skin the entire way. Nervously, I side-stepped out of his cocoon and his hand fell away.

Not a care in the world, Luke sighed. "Give us a second, Eddy."

Chet didn't say anything at first, but his nostrils slightly flared at Luke's shortening of his last name. His jaw ticked, then he nodded. "Of course."

He turned and stepped out of the room. Luke moved over and closed the door.

"Did you just metaphorically piss on my leg?" I questioned, aghast at his audacity.

He took a deep breath, ignored my question, and ran a hand over his face. "I have a feeling he's here to discuss what I came to tell you—before you distracted me."

"What?" I huffed indignantly. "I did no such thing!"

"Babe, you only have to breathe to distract me."

Burning like a flame, I knew my face was red at his admission. Part of the reason was that he did the same thing to me.

He briefly told me about the developments with Danielle. "When asshole Eddy comes in, you can't let on that you know."

Unable to get past what he'd told me, and knowing he'd likely held back some of the details, I started to cry.

"I'm so sorry. I wish this wasn't the news I had for you." He used his thumb to wipe away my tears, then reluctantly opened the door for Chet, but kept a supportive arm around me when the police officer came in.

"I'm very sorry to interrupt," Chet said with what seemed like a bit of an attitude. "I didn't realize you were busy."

"Oh! Um, Luke and I were just going over details for the fundraiser," I stammered.

Luke glared at me, then Officer Edwards.

"Could I speak to you—alone?" he asked me as he shot daggers at Luke. The tension in the room was damn near palpable. They were like two dogs squaring off before lunging at each other.

"No," Luke bluntly replied before I could answer.

My eyes flashed to him in question, but he was holding Chet's gaze.

After clearing his throat, Chet spoke but met only my eyes, effectively ignoring Luke's presence.

"I thought you might like to know they found what they believe to be Danielle's body, and I wanted to see if anyone had remembered any other details from the day she disappeared." Chet lifted his chin slightly as he finished.

Though Luke had given me a heads-up, he'd said not to give away that I already knew. Playing my part well, I acted surprised. My gasp of horror, however, was real. It wouldn't matter how many times I was told she was gone; I'd forever be dismayed by the event. A chill rippled across my cheeks and down to my toes.

"Shouldn't one of the detectives have come by to speak to Ms. Monroe?" Luke asked, brow cocked as he crossed his arms.

I couldn't be certain, but Chet seemed to get red in the neck. "The detective is busy, and I said I'd come by," he said through gritted teeth. "Since I'd be in the area on my patrol anyway."

Luke didn't reply; he simply stared coldly at the other man.

After a moment of confused and emotional silence, I took a shaky breath and interrupted their pissing contest with my reply. "No. No one has said anything to me about seeing or remembering anything from that day."

"I'm sorry to have bothered you, Ms. Monroe. Because of the delicate nature of the case, I'd appreciate it if you kept this knowledge to yourself for now. I'll be in touch." His eyes cut to Luke, who completely snubbed him. Honestly, I was surprised he didn't flip Chet off.

As soon as we heard the main door close, Luke enveloped me against his body and pulled out his phone. "Find out why that fucker Eddy was over here telling Hailey they found Danielle," he barked into the device.

Confused, I drew back to look at him with a frown.

He spoke to the other party for a few minutes, but his side of the conversation was stilted. After he ended the call, he pressed his thumb and middle finger into the inside corners of his closed eyes.

"Will you be okay today?" he asked.

I nodded, though I was sickened by the loss of Danielle.

"Look, I need to know if we're still good. If you've met

someone who gives you something I'm not able to, just let me know. I promised you I'd be monogamous, but that goes both ways," he rumbled.

"What are you talking about? What would give you the idea I'd been with someone else?" I demanded as I stepped back out of his hold and wiped away a stray tear. My arms crossed defensively.

"You haven't been home the last two nights," he said, his jaw muscle jumping as he seemed to stare into my damn soul.

With an indignant scoff, I gave him an incredulous glare. "Not that it's your business, but I was at my girlfriend's place the night you were 'too busy' for me, and last night I was home sick."

His eyes closed, and his face pinched before he ran a hand roughly over it. "Right. Now I feel like a dick. I'm sorry, I tried to stop by both nights, but the first night you didn't answer, and last night, your place looked deserted."

Something ridiculous bubbled up within me, and I found myself smiling like an idiot while I still experienced residual sniffles. "You stopped by both nights?"

"Yeah," he gruffly admitted. The truth of what he was implying hit me.

"You were jealous," I said in wonder as he scraped his teeth over his bottom lip and turned his attention out the window.

"No, I wasn't. I just wanted to make sure we were still on the same page. But I need to get going. Will you be home tonight?" he grumbled. He raked his fingers through his hair, causing his bicep to bulge and the vein that ran down the center to pop out.

Trying not to drool at the way his muscles moved under his inked skin, I nodded with a watery but wondrous smile.

"Cool. See you then?" He waited for me to reply.

"Of course," I assured him before biting my bottom lip.

He looked like he was going to say something and made a move like he was coming toward me, but stopped himself. The muscle in his jaw jumped as he visibly ground his teeth. Then he spun on his heel and left.

When my knees could no longer hold me, I fell to my chair, blew my nose, and stared into space, overwhelmed by the information that had been dropped on me. There had been bad and good, but neither really balanced the other.

Taking a deep breath, I tried to tell myself it did no good to worry over things I couldn't change, yet I did it anyway. The safety of the other residents was on my mind. I would do whatever was necessary to keep the children in my charge safe.

Yet, despite the horrible news Chet delivered, I found myself with a dreamy smile off and on throughout the day. The revelation of Luke being jealous was the cause.

I refused to acknowledge why that made me giddy.

Oh, who was I kidding; my feelings were getting involved, and I damn well knew it.

In a nutshell, I was screwed.

Chapter
TWELVE

Snow

"CARRIED AWAY"—SHINEDOWN

A week after Officer Dickwad Edwards delivered the shitty news to Hailey, all hell broke loose.

"Boss, you better come out here." Reaper stuck his head in my office door. The expression on his face told me it wasn't good.

"What's up?" I warily asked as I stood.

"Cops are here," he said with a frown.

"Jesus, now what?" I groaned.

We moved quickly down the hall and out to the common

area. Several officers, including Dickhead Edwards, were waiting with their hands resting threateningly on their service weapons.

"To what do I owe this lovely visit?" I sarcastically questioned.

"We have a warrant to search the premises," Edwards all but sneered.

"On what grounds?" I demanded.

"On these grounds," he replied as he shoved the paperwork in my hand and instructed his cronies to leave nothing unturned. My teeth gritted as I read the bullshit warrant. There was no way.

"That's absolute shit, and you know it. We had nothing to do with Danielle, and you won't find any of that," I argued, flicking my hand to hit the papers.

"Well, I guess we'll see, now won't we," he said with a snarky smile. It didn't last long, because it dropped when he snarled to his fellow officers, "Search them."

We were all patted down like common criminals and our weapons secured out of our reach.

"Get Ryland on the phone. Now," I told Vinny.

He nodded and pulled out his phone to call our attorney.

When one of the officers opened a knife and made a motion to stab the couch cushion, I stepped forward.

"What the fuck? No way. That's completely unnecessary."

Officer Dickwad raised a brow and shot me a triumphant grin. "Are you refusing our search? Trying to impede a police investigation? Because if so, that's obstruction of justice."

He knew damn well he had me. "You can't maliciously destroy our property or your search can be deemed invalid and anything you find can't be used against us," I added through gritted teeth. I wasn't an idiot, and I knew a little something about the law.

He stepped up until we were nearly toe to toe. "Prove it."

Rage building in me, I watched with clenched fists as they destroyed the clubhouse. Sliced open the couches and table benches. Turned the furniture over. Broke the liquor bottles when they swiped them off the shelves.

Tash startled and let out a brief shriek at the sound of the glass breaking. Soap wrapped an arm around her as he buried her face in his shoulder.

When they moved down the hall toward our rooms, Reaper turned to me, chest heaving. "This is fucking bullshit, Prez."

"I'm fully aware," I ground out.

One of the assholes called out for Edwards from down the hall. Chet sauntered down to see what his crony wanted. Then he turned my way with a sardonic rise of his brow.

"Whose room is this?" he called out as he pointed into one of the doorways.

"Two-Speed, that's your room, isn't it?" Apollo said through clenched teeth. He'd about come unglued when they ransacked the infirmary.

"Yeah," Two-Speed replied cautiously with a questioning frown.

Edwards and the other officer approached us with a plastic bag. Within it was what looked like blue fabric.

"What the hell is that?" I asked, but the douchebags ignored me.

Edwards announced they were arresting Two-Speed for the disappearance of Danielle DeSilva, then began reading him his rights and spun him against the wall. The cop slapped cuffs on him as he smashed Two-Speed into the wall.

"That was borderline police brutality. He's not fighting you," I growled. Two-Speed shot me a look that was full of anger mixed with a flicker of fear.

"Don't worry, brother. I'll deal with this. Say nothing. I'll have Ryland meet you at the station," I promised. As they pushed Two-Speed to get him moving, I turned to Vinny. He was holding on to his temper as tenuously as I was.

"None of you leave town, now! You hear?" Edwards called out with a grin. His chin rose as he gave me a look that screamed "Got you."

When the last asshole in blue exited the building, we began to clean up the mess. "Reaper! Call Hacker! Find out if that shit recorded."

"Sure as fuck will," he replied with a curl of his lip.

"Good. Tell him we need it downloaded to give to Ryland." Reaper nodded and headed to Hacker's room. It was really nothing more than an office now that he and Kassi had bought a house together.

It wasn't long before Kent Ryland was walking through the door. His dark gaze swept over the mess we were slowly cleaning up.

"Jesus. What exactly did they think they were going to find here?" he asked as his gaze swept the room. "I hope someone recorded this shit."

"I'm waiting for Hacker to get here, but I'm sure we got it on video. Come back to my office, and I'll fill you in," I said as I handed off the contractor bag I'd been filling to Hollywood. Not waiting to see if Ryland followed me, I stormed to my office.

Vinny and I stood the chairs up, then filled Ryland in on what we knew. Our attorney quietly took notes as he listened to everything we said. He asked us a few questions, made a few notes, then closed his notebook.

"I'll get on this. You think he's guilty?" Ryland asked me as he held my gaze.

"Not a chance," I insisted. Two-Speed was crazy as hell, but not like that. He'd gotten his road name because he only knew two speeds—slow and warp speed.

"You think they planted that shit." It wasn't a question. Ryland waited for me to confirm.

"Has to be. Everything is too convenient. They had a warrant specifically for personal items belonging to Danielle DeSilva." I sighed.

"The question is why?" Ryland sat back in his chair.

"Why? Because they have a hard-on for us about a mile long. Who better to pin shit on?" I spat in disgust. No matter how cut-and-dried it seemed, something was off.

"But at the expense of letting the real perpetrator go free?" Vinny quietly questioned. He made sense.

"Unless they know who it is and they're trying to protect them," I reasoned as I met Ryland's steady stare.

"That's exactly what I was thinking. This could get ugly," Ryland said as he put his notebook back into his briefcase and stood. Vinny and I followed suit. "I'm going to get on this. There's no way they're getting away with blatant destruction of property.

Your boy knows not to say anything to them until I get there, right?"

I nodded.

"Perfect. Then I'll head on over." He shook our hands, and we showed him out, dodging the rubble left behind from the search.

Once he was out the door, I called everyone to church. "Twenty minutes. Get Joker here from the tattoo shop. I don't care if he's in the middle of tattooing the queen's ass. Hacker had an install today. Did he answer?" I asked Reaper when I stuck my head in Hacker's "war room."

"Yeah, he did."

"Good. Call him back. See if he's finished; if not, he can go back tomorrow. I want everyone present."

"Roger that," said Reaper as he pulled out his phone.

Vinny and I went into the chapel and began righting the table and chairs. We also checked everything for possible surveillance devices. I'd have Hacker run a bug check when he got back.

"Why the fuck did they have to tip over the table? This thing is heavy as fuck," Vinny grumbled as we lifted it up to its legs.

"Because Edwards is a dick and a half," I replied, not caring if there was a listening device. I hated that guy.

Reaper walked in and started grabbing chairs with us. "Joker's on his way. Hacker was already heading back."

"Good."

One by one, the members of the Demented Sons filed into the chapel. Each of them took his seat. My eyes traveled the room, taking in my brothers.

Vinny, Cash, Dice, Reaper, Hollywood, Hacker, Joker, Smokey, Blue, Soap, and Apollo. "Call the prospect in here for this. Hacker, sweep the room." I didn't need to explain further—he knew what I was asking for and immediately complied.

"We're good. At least in here. I'll check the rest of the club-house when we're done," Hacker informed me, and I nodded with satisfaction.

Normally we wouldn't include a prospect, but I wanted everyone informed. If the guy made the cut, we'd already decided on his road name. Reload, because he carried at least four loaded magazines with him everywhere he went.

He followed Reaper back into the room and leaned against the wall. Reaper closed the door after he was inside.

"You probably all know, but Two-Speed was arrested." There was muttering from every member. "Quiet! We all know it's bull-shit. I want to know where every single one of you was during the time that the girl disappeared. Not because I think any of you are guilty, but we need to verify alibis."

For the next hour, we hashed out where everyone was during the time in question. Everyone had a rock-solid alibi except Dice and Vinny. Theirs were questionable for part of the time, but likely not long enough to allow them to look guilty. Then again, it seemed like the cops were trying to set us up for the shit, so who knew what the fuckers would do.

"Ryland will work out Two-Speed's whereabouts at the time. No one goes anywhere alone. Make sure you can always verify who you were with, when, and where. I'm not sure why they're trying to pin this shit on us, but we're gonna find out. We're also gonna step up our game on finding out what happened with Danielle." Every brother steadily held my gaze.

"Also, there was another overdose last week. It was down

near Graettinger, but that's still in our radius. Look into the details for me," I instructed Hacker.

"Roger that," he replied.

After I banged the gavel, the chairs scraped the floor as everyone stood. They quietly left the room, but I stayed seated. Lost in thought, I didn't realize anyone was in the room until someone cleared their throat. Pulled out of my head, my gaze darted to where Reaper stood waiting.

"You need something?"

He glanced over his shoulder to ensure we were alone. When he was satisfied we were, he spoke quietly. "I'm not tryin' to tell you your business, boss, but with all this going on, you might need to give Ms. Monroe a heads-up. Before she hears this bullshit from somewhere else."

"Why would you say that?"

"Well, you've been working with her on the fundraiser, and, well, you know… people talk." He shuffled from one foot to the other as he shoved his hands in his back pockets and shrugged.

"About?" I knew, but I wasn't going to admit it.

"You and her," he hedged.

"There is no me and her," I insisted—because I knew I'd have to step back until we figured this shit out. There was no way I was dragging her into this mess. She had enough to worry about.

The idea didn't sit well with my cock, but I needed to think with the right damn head. No matter how much it pissed me off.

He thinned his lips and raised his brows like he didn't believe me.

"Whatever you say, boss man. I'm out," he told me and left. Nervously tapping my fingers on the dark wood, I procrastinated composing the message I knew I needed to send. The thought of not feeling the silky glide of her skin against mine sucked. As much as not hearing her voice, or holding her close. Though I knew it was the right thing to do, actually making that move made my chest cramp. Absently, I rubbed it with my knuckles.

Then I got up, grabbed my phone from the basket outside the chapel door, and sat back down. Though I knew what needed to be done, I needed to see her one last time.

It was time to say goodbye.

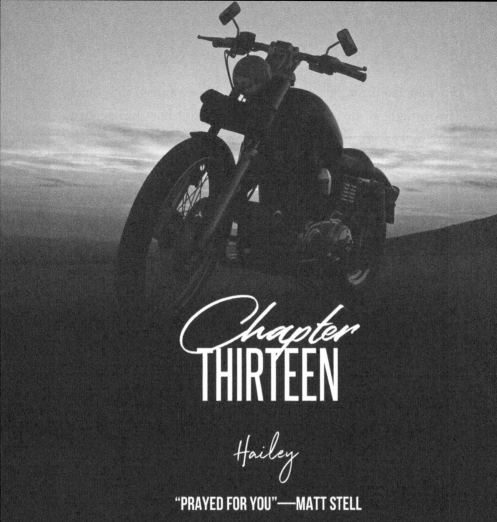

Chapter THIRTEEN

Hailey

"PRAYED FOR YOU"—MATT STELL

"Mr. Matthews is here," Alba announced over my intercom.

"Thank you, Alba. Send him back. If you have everything caught up, feel free to head home. I'll lock up." My cheeks heated when I thought I heard her chuckle before she ended the connection.

It had been over three months since Luke had walked into my office and blown my well-organized life to smithereens. Three months since we decided to have a no-strings-attached casual-sex relationship.

A perfect friends-with-benefits situation. Except I saw how well that worked out for my college friend Tawny. She and Roman had started with the same type of agreement. They were getting married soon.

Telling myself our situation was different, I sighed. Luke was an incredible lover, but I appreciated that he respected my need for space. I was busy, and at twenty-nine, I was proud of what I'd accomplished.

I'd worked hard, sacrificing a lot over the years to get to where I was. While most of my childhood and college friends had husbands and families, I'd worked sometimes seven days a week. Sure, there were times I had that pang in my chest for something I couldn't put a name to, but I was essentially happy.

Wasn't I?

My parents had come for a visit, and I'd had to sneak out in the night to meet up with him in my backyard. Going without him for a week was a hard pass. Not that my parents were prudes, but I wasn't ready to discuss my sex life with them. If my mother got a single whiff of potential grandchildren, she'd be relentless. Luke and I had christened my gazebo like rock stars.

A smile curled my lips at the memory.

"Must be a pretty good thought." His voice rumbled from the door. Leaning against the frame, his eyes traced every inch of me. From the heat in his gaze, I knew he was stripping me in his mind.

"Very," I replied with a saucy grin.

He came in and closed the door. Then he leaned over my desk to kiss me. It was sultry and full of promise. When it hit me that it was very couple-ish behavior, I broke away, licked my lips, and cleared my throat.

"The guys have almost everything assembled for tomorrow." We had decided to advertise not only on social media but in a larger radius to maximize attendance. Luke's club donated all the labor for setup and the funds for the prizes. We were doing a carnival theme this year. The club had also footed the bill for a few carnival rides. It was above and beyond, and I knew it would be a success.

"Thank you. I still can't get over how much you guys donate to keep this tradition in place. It's pretty impressive."

"We love doing it, and it's for a great cause," he said with a smile, but the mischievous light in his eyes dimmed a little, stoking my curiosity.

"Everything okay?" I asked, suddenly sobered.

"Yeah. It's just rough sometimes."

"Because of your brother?" I questioned.

"Yeah."

"Trust me, I feel you," I offered, because I did. If there had been any way for me to turn back the clock and try again with my sister, I would.

"Is that why you got into adolescent drug rehab?" he asked as he sat on the edge of my desk and rested his hands on his thigh.

My heart clenched a little, and I sighed. "Yes. It is."

Sensing my need to gather my feelings, he didn't ask anything further. Then again, maybe he was dealing with corralling his own demons about his brother. It was hell losing someone close to you to drugs or the life path those drugs led you down.

"Not only the awful situation with Danielle; did you hear

there was another overdose from that crazy-ass drug?" I asked him in an attempt to divert the subject. If his expression had dimmed before, it damn near enraged at that. I was instantly sorry I brought it up.

"Yes, and the people responsible keep slipping through the cracks," he ground out. "I heard one of the kids was using that before he entered the program here. The police talked to him about where he'd gotten it, but buying drugs has entered the digital age. They don't know any names; it's all electronic transfer of funds with no proof of what the transaction was for. Pickup is sometimes in person, sometimes via a middleman, sometimes in a gym locker."

His expression quickly shut down.

"How do you know what the police found out?" I frowned. I hadn't heard all of that.

He shrugged. "They published some of it in the news and on their social media page."

The wheels in my head spun as I thought about the biker show I'd watched. Though Luke had laughingly said they were nothing like that, I had to wonder. Wouldn't a criminal deny everything they did?

Deciding to let it lie, I pulled up the projections to go over with him. "So, it looks like the number of advance tickets purchased this year is exceeding the past two years by about 20 percent. That's pretty amazing."

"Good, I'm glad to hear that."

We went over a few last-minute details before I locked up my office and he walked me to my car. Upon reaching my door, I spun to face him.

"You know that everyone thinks there's something going on between us," I said.

He chuckled. "Well, there is. It's a small town; I figured it was no secret."

"That doesn't bother you?"

"Should it?"

"Well, I'm worried about what people will say." I'd really thought we could keep it a secret, but I'd screwed up and fallen asleep at his house that morning. When I'd snuck out in my walk of shame the next morning, his neighbor—Alba's *mother*—was outside with her yappy little dog.

Since the fateful neighbor day, I was sure she'd run her mouth to more than Justine. I'd been getting lots of sidelong glances—some judging and some jealous. Not that it had stopped me from hooking up with him. I had no self-control when it came to the gorgeous, broody biker.

Which made me admit I hadn't stayed as detached as I'd insisted I would.

"You mean what they're already saying? Come on, Hailey; you can't be that naive. You have to know that they're already saying what they're gonna say. Are you trying to tell me you want to call this off? Because of a little gossip?" Disbelief colored his gaze before he winced.

Burying my face in my hands, I groaned. "I don't knowwwww."

When he didn't say anything, I peeked between my fingers. He appeared thoughtful and slightly irritated. "You know what? You're right. This is a bad idea. If there's anything else you need before tomorrow, let me know. I'll see you around."

Incredulous, I dropped my hands to watch him walk over to his bike. Not once did he give me a backward glance before he roared out of the parking lot.

"Dammit."

The sound of carnival music and laughter filled the air. Ticket sales had far exceeded our expectations, and people were still buying them the day of the event. The scent of carnival food teased me, and my stomach rumbled.

It was late, and I hadn't eaten all day.

"This appears to be a huge hit," Polly said from behind me. Surprise had me spinning in her direction. I hadn't been expecting her to come, since she was still recuperating from her second hip surgery.

"Thank you. I was worried I wouldn't be able to do the Leon justice, with it being my first year." A relieved smile spread over my face.

"I knew you'd do just fine." She returned my smile, then appeared contemplative. "So, what's the scoop with you and Luke Matthews?"

My heart hammered at the mention of his name. I'd seen him arrive with his club brothers earlier, but he hadn't sought me out once. Despite the way my eyes followed him, not once did he glance my way.

"It would appear there isn't one," I softly replied as I caught a glimpse of him through the crowd with a dark-haired woman clinging to his arm. Polly followed my line of sight and took a deep breath before heavily exhaling.

"Luke is a complicated man. He doesn't believe he deserves a happily ever after. I was hoping you might be the one to prove him wrong."

I sighed. "Well, I'm sorry to disappoint you, Polly, but I don't think it's in the cards. It was never like that anyway," I insisted. The truth hurt my heart, and I had to admit I'd completely failed at staying disconnected.

She gave a snort and paused as if she was going to say something. Then she patted my arm and slowly made her way over to her husband, who was helping their grandchildren with the duck pond.

"Girl, why are you being so damn stubborn?" Justine sidled up next to me as she shoved kettle corn in her mouth.

"Gimme some of that," I said as I shoved my hand in her bag. "I'm not. Besides, he obviously didn't wait around for me for very long." Completely unladylike, I spoke around the delicious salty-sweetness I was devouring.

"Hmm, well, you could always go rip out her extensions and demand she leave your man alone. That's what I'd do," Justine helpfully supplied before dumping more food in her mouth. I rolled my eyes. She would probably do it too.

Damn, I hated that he'd moved on in a fucking day. Sure, we weren't a couple, but I at least expected we were exclusive. The thought that maybe I'd been the only half of us that had been monogamous turned my hurt into anger. Jesus, I needed to go get tested if that was the case.

"Maybe I will," I said as I filled my face with another handful of popcorn. Yet, I stood rooted to the ground.

After three more helpings of Justine's kettle corn, I was about to go give him a piece of my mind when there was a shout. A boy of about fifteen or sixteen was racing into the crowd yelling for help.

"Please! Someone help my friend!" Eyes wide in terror, he cast his gaze helplessly around. Several of the town's firemen were there, and they hurried after the boy as he went back behind the amusement rides.

Worried, I raced after them.

When I pushed through the crowd, I saw several of them working on another boy. CPR in progress, they had serious expressions on their faces. "Someone call 911!" one of them shouted.

"On it!" I yelled; my phone was already ringing. When the 911 operator answered, the older fireman started to shout out information to me that I relayed to the dispatcher. Within seconds, I heard sirens drawing near.

The paramedics pushed through the crowd to take over. The firemen were filling them in as they continued to give alternating compressions and bag the unresponsive boy. Not stopping, they loaded him up in the ambulance. It wasn't long before they were tearing out of the lot, lights flashing and sirens blaring.

I glanced around for Luke. No matter how tough I liked to think I was and no matter that I'd pushed him away, I needed him.

When I didn't see him in the area, I pulled out my phone and called him.

"Hailey," he said, and I questioned whether he sounded happy to hear from me.

"Are you busy?" I asked, trying to keep my voice steady.

He hesitated, and I almost hung up. Images of what he could be doing with the brunette bombarded my imagination.

"A little. Can I meet you later at your place?"

I almost told him never mind, but my mouth and my brain weren't in sync. "Yes."

"Okay, see you as soon as I can get away."

"Sure," I said quietly and ended the call.

Glancing around, I felt my heart sink.

The mood had gone from jovial gaiety to somber silence in the blink of an eye. People started to quietly disperse, and most were leaving. Though the event had been close to wrapping up, I hated that it had ended this way. I was sick to my stomach for that kid. I dropped to a picnic table and held my head.

"Ms. Monroe?" a soft voice said, and I looked up. It was Gemma, one of the kids from our facility. Lynn, the tech assigned to the few kids who were at a point in their therapy where they had limited outings, was standing behind her. She whispered in Gemma's ear to encourage her to talk.

"What's wrong, Gemma?" I asked.

She bit her lip, gave a nervous glance to Lynn, then looked back at me.

"I overheard those boys talking when I was doing the ring toss." She swallowed hard. "They were talking about using something."

"Something?" I questioned cautiously.

"A special drug they had picked up," she admitted with worry in her eyes. She nervously wrung her hands.

"Shit," I heard and whipped my attention to where the voice had come from. Luke pulled out his phone and walked off, talking quietly. I was shocked because I thought he'd already left.

Needing to assure Gemma she wasn't in trouble, I dismissed

Luke from my thoughts for the moment and got up to walk around the table. I crouched in front of her to look her in the eye. "Did you have anything to do with them?"

Frantically, she shook her head. "No, ma'am! I swear!"

"Easy, I wasn't accusing you; I just wanted to make sure you were okay. You have nothing to worry about if you weren't involved, but the police may want to talk to you about what you overheard."

Tears welled in her eyes before spilling over when she blinked. With a sniffle, she nodded.

"Was there anyone else who was with you when you heard the boys talking?"

She nodded, then said it was two of the boys in her group.

"Lynn, could I please talk to them?"

She motioned over her shoulder to the rest of the kids from her group. They all stepped forward.

"Which one of you overheard those boys talking?" They all fidgeted nervously, but no one spoke up. Finally, Tommy, a boy with shaggy blond hair, nudged Julius, who glared at Tommy, then his shoulders slumped.

"I did," Julius admitted. "And so did Jose."

The volunteers were closing up and tearing down the various booths as the colored lights of the Ferris wheel blinked brightly. Knowing I should have them talk to the police, I pulled out my phone and the business card to call the officer who had arrived with the ambulance.

"What are you doing?" Julius asked with wide eyes.

"I'm calling the police officer so you can tell them what you know."

"No! No way! I ain't talkin' to no cops, Ms. Monroe. I didn't hear nothin' at all," he belligerently said with a defiant lift of his chin.

Frustrated, I set my phone down. "Okay, will you boys tell *me* what you saw or heard?"

They exchanged a glance, then met my gaze, then looked away. Finally, they reluctantly nodded.

I made sure the volunteers and the staff that were helping with teardown were okay, and I returned to the Leon to see what the boys had to say.

They spilled what they knew, and after puking in my trashcan, I sat there stunned long after they returned to their rooms for bed.

Chapter FOURTEEN

Snow

"HUSH"—HELLYEAH

Sitting at my desk, I was trying to make sense of today's events. What a shitty end to a shitty day.

Reaper stopped by. "You okay, boss?"

With a frown, I looked up from where I had been staring at, my fingers drumming on the desktop.

"No, but that doesn't seem to matter."

"Yeah, I know."

"Hacker have anything yet?"

He just shook his head and took a seat across from me.

I pulled out my bottle of whiskey and poured us both a shot. Irritation boiled in my guts at the dead ends we kept hitting.

All day I'd been agitated. Hailey hadn't called me last night, nor had she called at all today. I'd thought about going to talk to her at the fundraiser, but she always had someone with her. Though I tried not to be obvious, I hadn't been able to keep my gaze from straying to wherever she was in the crowd.

Then, I stubbornly reminded myself that this was what I wanted. Hell, I told her we were better off calling it quits. No way would I be the first to cave.

I didn't need her. She didn't need the potentially dangerous baggage that came with me and my club.

But fuck if I didn't want her.

Though I knew I needed to call things off, and she'd offered me the perfect opportunity to do so, I'd been on the verge of dragging her off somewhere quiet. At least until Sonja had come up, begging me to win her a stuffed bear or some shit. By the time I pawned her off on one of the other brothers, Hailey was talking with Polly.

Then I'd been stopped by a guy wanting to talk about bringing his classic Mustang in for a bunch of custom work. I'd barely finished talking to him when the kid had come running for help.

Shit had gone downhill from there.

By the time the paramedics drove off, everything had essentially ground to a halt, and I couldn't see Hailey anywhere.

When she called me, I was beyond shocked, but I didn't let on. It was the last thing I expected.

After I ended the brief call, I cursed. For the first time in my life, I wanted something more with a woman—one I didn't deserve. Cammie and I had been casual, and I was able to keep it that way. With Hailey, she'd gotten under my skin. So deeply that she haunted me—distracting me at every turn. When I closed my eyes at night, I saw her. My dreams were so fucking X-rated I was almost embarrassed the next day. She was a fever in my blood that nothing could cool. She sent fire through me with each touch, that left me craving her every minute of every motherfuckin' day.

It was all that and more that had me seeking her out after ending the call. That was when I overheard that kid telling her what they'd seen. I'd immediately made a call to Hacker, then Baker. Hacker and I had returned to the clubhouse to see what he could find on the kid that overdosed.

I'd been sitting at my desk simmering ever since.

"Prez, I got the toxicology report on that kid." Hacker stood in my office doorway. Reaper and I both glanced at him expectantly.

Motioning him in, I swallowed the shot I'd poured. Reaper did the same. "What does it say?"

But I knew before he told me.

"It's looking like it was Black Night," he said, confirming my suspicions.

"At a fucking fundraiser for a drug prevention and reha-bilitation center. Jesus," I said before raking a frustrated hand through my hair.

Hacker and Reaper both remained wisely silent.

"Did he make it?" I asked.

"Yeah, but he hasn't woken up yet."

"Did we talk to the other kid?"

"Yeah. Apollo knew the dad. Kid won't talk. Well, other than to insist he doesn't know where his friend got the shit from."

"So we have to wait for the kid to wake up?"

"Appears that way," he apologetically replied.

"Cops are gonna be waiting for that moment too," I said, then sighed. "Maybe it's time to pull in a favor. Is that all?"

"For now."

I waved him off and took another shot. Then I picked up the phone and hit send on a number I didn't relish calling for a favor.

"Snow," the deep voice drawled out the greeting.

"Venom."

"Now that we both know who we're talking to, why the fuck are you calling me on a Saturday night when I'm trying to get lucky with my ol' lady?" I heard Loralei squawk in the background. Venom chuckled.

Venom is the president of the Royal Bastards MC down in Ankeny. He'd also been my best friend growing up. It was because of him that I joined the military and pulled my shit together after my brother died.

I'd also helped him and his ol' lady when shit had gone crazy for her up here. Not that I was exactly keeping score, but it wasn't like I hadn't helped him at the drop of a hat. That's what friends did. Regardless of our club loyalties, we remained friends.

"I'm calling in one of those favors," I admitted as I slouched back in my chair and stared sightlessly at the ceiling.

His tone sobered immediately. "What's up?"

Hating that I hadn't been able to get to the bottom of this shit myself, I clenched my fist. Then I told him everything I knew. Once I was done, I waited. He blew out a hefty breath.

"Fucking hell. We've heard whispers of that shit being run by some scattered members of the Bloody Scorpions and some thugs that came from out of state. But so far, we've kept it out of this area. At least as far as we know. Damn, you'd think that would be more prevalent in a big city than up there. Wish we could figure out where that shit is coming from. Because unless we can do that, there isn't much we can do." He was silent for a moment. It didn't sit well with me that he was right—our hands were tied until we figured out who was supplying it.

"The problem is, there's not much for kids to do around here. Not a lot of jobs for teens. Not much of a future industry-wise. Kids are bored and restless. The pieces of shit peddling that crap prey on that fact."

"True. At least when we were kids, it was just beer around a bonfire on a Saturday night. Let me talk to the boys tomorrow morning and see what we dig up. If I have to, I'll see if Chains is willing to go up there and check things out."

"I appreciate it." They had a few more connections and, um, other advantages that most people didn't know about. Things I didn't tell my own brothers about.

"Now, if you don't mind, I have a woman to ravish."

I gave a half-hearted laugh. "Well, thanks for answering my call."

His tone went serious. "Anytime, brother. And I mean that."

"I know."

We ended the call, and I sat alone in silence. My mind wouldn't shut off though. I kept going over and over everything we knew—which wasn't much. Then it wandered to Hailey. Staring at my phone, I debated calling her and canceling. Now that shit was seriously heating up, I needed to ensure Hailey was nowhere around me or any of the shitstorm that was brewing.

Knowing I'd cave if I heard her voice, I sent a text instead.

Me: Some things came up. I won't be able to stop by to see you.

The little dots danced on my screen, disappeared, then reappeared.

Hailey: Okay? I probably won't be able to sleep.

Hailey: If you want to stop by when you're done.

More than anything, I wanted to ask her if that meant she was ready to admit it didn't matter what the town busybodies said. Except I knew that wasn't conducive to what needed to be done.

Me: Probably not a good idea.

Hailey: Do you want to go over the final numbers from the event tomorrow?

Me: No. I'm going to be tied up for a while. This isn't working for me anymore. I'm sorry. If there's any issues, you can contact my VP Vinny.

The words made me feel physically ill. The last thing I wanted was to end things with her. Knowing it was the right thing to do, no matter how much I disliked it, I sent her his contact information. My teeth ground as I thought about her talking to Vinny. For a few minutes, there was no further communication. Then her next text made me wince.

Hailey: Fine.

Venom had come through in spades.

"Fuck you!" the little punk tied to the chair spat, remaining stubborn.

"No, thanks. You're not my type," Soap said before he planted his fist in the guy's eye. Though I already knew it, I didn't give a shit what his name was.

I'd give the puny pissant credit—he'd lasted much longer than I'd thought he would. Soap was a big bastard, and I knew his meaty fists had to pack a wallop. The guy had to be feeling it.

"Now, I'm going to ask you again, Stuart… where are you getting the product from?" Soap quietly demanded.

"Fuck—" But the guy didn't get the chance to finish his thought because Soap pressed a pistol to his head.

"Fuck this shit, P. Let me just shoot him. We can pick up the other guy and get answers from him," Soap growled. There was no other guy, but we waited to see if the battered asshole in the chair took the bait.

Soap cocked the pistol. The sound echoed loudly in the underground space. The asshole pissed himself. My nose curled slightly at the smell of urine mixed with blood.

"Wait! Hold on; let's not be rash!" he begged in a suddenly whiny voice.

"Give us something, or I let my friend here blow your brains across the room," I said in a sinister whisper.

"Hugo. The guy's name is Hugo," he whimpered.

"Hugo, who?" I demanded.

"All I know is Hugo! I message him when I need another batch. Once a month he sends me a new number with a random area code, so I don't know where he is exactly."

"Boss man?" Soap questioned.

"Get his phone," I ordered Joker. He grabbed it from the pile of the dude's shit and handed it to me.

"What's he saved as?"

"Hugo Boss," the guy muttered. I looked up from his phone and gave him an are-you-serious gaze.

"This is how things are gonna play out. I'm gonna dial your good friend Hugo. You're gonna tell him you need another shipment." Unwavering, my gaze held his.

"But I just got one," he started to argue.

"Shut the fuck up and listen to me," I said with exaggerated patience. Something I didn't have much of at that point. "You had a boom this month. Sold out like it was a chance at Willy Wonka's last golden ticket. You need a refill."

"But—" Soap smacked him like a bitch.

"What part of shut the fuck up didn't you understand?" he asked the guy.

We told him what he needed to know about the plan. What we didn't tell him was that Venom's boys were waiting on standby for cleanup and disposal of his ass once we had what we wanted. Piece of shit was selling that shit to fucking kids as young as eleven. What kind of morally reprehensible dickwad did shit like that? Without remorse, even.

"Now, do you understand? Nod if you do." I slowly enunciated every syllable. The guy furiously nodded.

"Remember, he gets suspicious in any way and my friend here is gonna cut your fingers off one by one, then shoot your dick off." The pussy whimpered and nodded again.

I dialed the number and put the phone on speaker.

"Why are you calling me? You just got the black hoodies you ordered," the mechanically distorted voice came through the speaker.

Stuart did as he was told, and by the time the call ended, we had a meetup scheduled for the next week to get another shipment of "black hoodies."

Asshole played it off like a pro; I had to give him credit.

"Toss him in the cage."

He was yelling as I walked out of the dank cellar. Dumb fucker actually thought we were going to let him go and risk him running. Not happening.

Now we simply had to bide our time until next week.

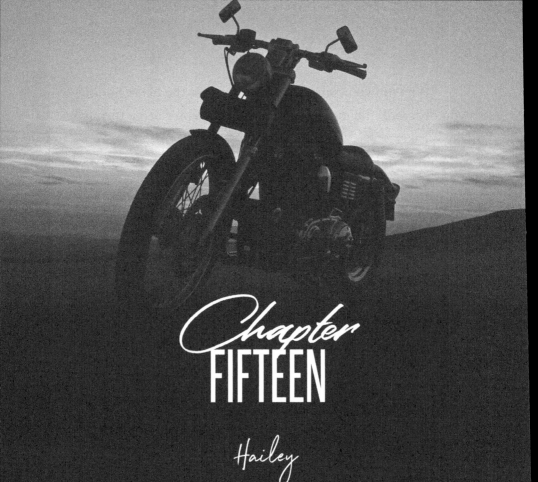

Chapter
FIFTEEN

Hailey

"50 SHADES OF CRAZY"—CHASE RICE

"I WAS SURPRISED TO HEAR FROM YOU," MY DATE SAID WITH a smirk.

"Well, as you know, it's been a really busy few months. My mom got hurt, then I've been working insanely long hours after—well, there's simply been no time for myself at all. Things have finally settled down, I hope." I gave him what I hoped was an innocent smile.

"Honestly? I thought you were seeing Luke Matthews," he said before taking a sip of his drink.

My lips flattened as I held in my emotions. Then I flatly replied, "No."

"My mistake," he said with a crooked grin.

That out of the way, I encouraged him to prattle on about himself, since he was so good at it.

While we ate, I pretended to drink copious amounts of alcohol. Little did he know, I'd ordered a Sprite before he arrived. Then when the waiter came by, I simply requested another of the same on my own tab.

"Your job must be sooooo fascinating!" I simpered. Inside my head, I was making the universal gag motion.

He preened as he rubbed his jaw. For about the eighteenth time since we'd met at the restaurant, he stared at my cleavage. Exactly as I planned when I wore the low-cut, clingy sweater dress.

"Ms. Monroe." My back stiffened at the sound of Luke's voice.

Shit.

Shit.

Shit.

"Uh, hello, Mr. Matthews," I replied with a falsely bright smile. From the corner of my eye, I saw my date lean back in his seat, one hand loosely holding his glass.

"Imagine seeing you here—with Officer Edwards, no less. I wasn't aware that you knew each other like this," he said in a deceptively calm voice. The fury in his eyes belied his words and tone.

A quick glance at Chet revealed his narrowed gaze flashing back and forth between me and Luke. His shoulders had tensed, and he had a white-knuckle grip on his fork.

Inside, I screamed at Luke, *Why do you care? You didn't want me!*

Purposely ignoring his comment, I took a sip of my drink. Then it occurred to me that we were at a nice restaurant over at the lakes. "And who are you with tonight?" I asked in a manner that projected innocent curiosity as I screamed inside.

"Luke, there you are. When I came out of the restroom, you were gone," a woman said from behind him. My own anger flared until he stepped to the side.

"Mom, I'd like you to meet Ms. Monroe from the Leon Adolescent Center."

Oh my God. His mother!

The woman smiled warmly. "My name is Mary," she said as she reached out to shake my hand. Her eyes were the same dark blue as her son's, and it was obvious he had his mother's cheekbones. "Thank you so much for what you do there."

She seemed to blink away tears.

My cheeks heated with embarrassment that I'd been jealous when I thought he was on a date. Then again, for all intents and purposes, that's what I looked like I was doing.

Awkwardness engulfed me, and I had to remind myself that he'd essentially walked away from us and whatever we'd had. Granted, thanks to my stubborn pride, I hadn't reached out to him in over a week either. Not that I hadn't wanted to.

"Well, we should probably get going and let Ms. Monroe get back to her *date*," he said with a slight sneer. "You two enjoy yourselves."

"Good night, and it was nice meeting you," Mary said over her shoulder as she rushed to catch up to her son. He moved with such masculine grace, he reminded me of a panther prowling through his domain.

More than anything, I wanted to run after him to tell him this wasn't what it seemed, but that would shoot all my careful planning to shit. I needed to focus. I also needed to remember he was the one who had ended things.

"So what exactly is your connection to Luke Matthews if you weren't dating?" Chet asked the question as if it was idle curiosity, but the tenseness hadn't left his shoulders. If everyone else in town had their tongues wagging about me and Luke, I was sure he'd heard the rumors.

"We went out once. It didn't work out. So we simply worked together on the planning for the annual fundraiser. As you probably know, his club was a huge contributor to its inception. You're also probably aware they make a significant donation each year in both time and money." I sipped my drink as if I wasn't bothered by the query in the least.

He snorted softly. "You mean his gang of thugs and their dirty money?"

Frowning at his bitter tone, I shrugged. "I'm not really that familiar with them outside the fundraiser." *Lies!*

I was so familiar with Luke Matthews, I could draw him from memory—that was, if I could draw anything outside of a stick figure. Regardless, I remembered every inch of him and what he could do to me. His brothers seemed like scary but good guys. I'd interacted with them a lot during the setup for the fundraiser.

"Well, it might be a good idea to steer clear of him and his gang of merry misfits. They're all trouble, and I'd hate to see you get tied up in that," he said before he wiped his mouth with the cloth napkin.

"Oh!" I tried for wide-eyed innocence again. "Have you known him long, then?"

"My whole life. He was older than me though. I went to school with his brother."

"I see. Well, I'll certainly keep that in mind, though I doubt our paths will cross outside of the annual fundraiser. Well, and occasionally running into each other in restaurants, it would seem." Another artificial smile, and one last sip of my beverage.

The waiter came by, and Chet gave him his credit card. I insisted on paying for my "bar tab."

"Well, it's getting late. I suppose we should call it a night," I said after he paid the bill. When I stood, I made a production of being unsteady. Pushing my boobs together as I leaned forward on the table to catch my balance, I gasped.

"Oh! Goodness," I said as I blinked innocently. Of course, his eyes were focused on my display of cleavage again. I wanted to smirk at how predictable he was.

"Let me walk you out," he said as he clasped my elbow in a firm grip. He walked me to my car but placed a hand on my arm when I went to open my door.

"As an officer of the law, it wouldn't be prudent of me to let a lady drive home after several mixed drinks."

"I'm not drunk," I insisted. Little did he know, that was an absolute truth.

"Maybe not blackout drunk, but you probably shouldn't be driving. Let me give you a ride home," he smoothly insisted.

"Are you sure?" I asked, faking concern and appreciation.

"Absolutely, and if you can't get a ride over to pick up your car tomorrow, I'll be happy to drive you back here."

"Oh, thank you so much." I gripped my purse tightly and threw my arms around him, smashing my boobs into his chest. I wanted to cringe when his hand slid from my back to rest on the top of my ass.

We were halfway back to Grantsville when he briefly glanced my way. "Since I'm driving, could I interest you in stopping by my place for a glass of wine? It's not really all that late, so I thought we could maybe relax, talk, then I could run you home."

"That sounds lovely. Thank you," I said with a doe-eyed gaze.

He lived in a newer neighborhood in a beautiful home. It was impressive. He left his car parked in the driveway and ushered me inside.

While I waited on the couch, I checked out the living room. Hardwood floors, massive stone fireplace, vaulted ceiling, with the upstairs looking down on the entire area. It seemed like a really expensive home for a small-town cop.

Spinning to face him as I heard him return, I pasted a smile on my face as he set the glasses on a dark wood coffee table. After efficiently removing the cork, he poured the bloodred wine in each glass until they were half-full.

With what I assumed he thought was a sultry look, he handed me my glass. "To new beginnings," he said as he held his glass to mine.

"To new beginnings," I repeated. My glass gave a crystal ping when they met, and I took a small sip after swirling it gently in my glass and sniffing it properly. At least I thought that's what I was supposed to do. A wine aficionado, I was not.

I sat on the couch, placed my purse next to me, and slowly crossed my legs. "You have a beautiful home," I offered.

"Thank you." He appeared somewhat distraught before he added, "My parents passed away several years ago. I was only able to buy this home because of their passing. It doesn't seem right, but I'm thankful for their thoughtfulness every day."

"I'm so sorry!" I earnestly replied. Well, maybe that explained that.

"It's okay. Like I said, it's been several years, but I still miss them every day."

Moving to set my glass on the table, I caught the base on the edge of the table. Red wine spilled across the dark wood and onto the floor. "Oh my God, I'm so sorry!"

"It's okay; I've got it." He set his glass on the dry end of the table and went to the kitchen. Watching over my shoulder, I dug in my purse and pulled out the small vial.

What I was doing was highly illegal, and I questioned the morality of it for a brief moment. Quickly dismissing my worries, I shook the powder into his glass and swirled it. Sweat ran down my back when the powder was still slightly visible. Unsure of what to do, I stirred it with my finger.

His returning footsteps drew closer as I watched the wine still moving in his glass. Heart pounding, I nervously glanced from the wine to his approach.

"Here! Let me do it. I made the mess." I stood up, stepping in front of his glass and reaching for the towel. I covertly wiped my finger on it.

He grinned. "It's okay. I'm not going to have a lady on her hands and knees cleaning my house."

128

The look in his eyes said he'd certainly like said lady on her knees for other things. A shiver of distaste shot through me. Honest to God, he hadn't done a lot that was extremely cringe-worthy, but it was a gut feeling. That topped with what the kids had told me had my hairs standing on end.

Once he mopped up the mess and wiped it down with the damp end of the towel, he left it sitting on the edge of the table. "More wine?" he asked with a smirk.

"Please," I said with a thankful smile. "And again, I'm so sorry I was such a klutz."

"It's fine. Accidents happen," he assured me.

After refilling my glass, he picked his up again. It took everything in me not to stare at him as he drank from the tainted wine. I had no idea if he'd be able to taste it or not, and my hands were getting clammy as I fought to appear normal and relaxed.

"This is fantastic," I complimented as I took another sip and met his gaze over the rim.

He cleared his throat and shifted on the couch, bringing his leg against mine. My breath caught, and I knew any second he'd call me out for what I'd done. Nervously, I took a bigger sip.

"What do you say we finish this wine and maybe… engage in some—" I licked the wine from my lower lip. "—evening activities?" My voice came across as breathless, though it was far from being passion related.

His mouth kicked up, and he downed the rest of his glass. Without another word, he stood and reached out for my hand. I gulped the rest of mine for courage, then set the empty glass with his.

Before placing my damp hand in his, I surreptitiously wiped the sweat from them on my dress.

Legs shaking, I followed him hand in hand to what was obviously the master bedroom. The entire way, I prayed that the research I'd done was accurate. I needed to get him on the bed because I had no idea how long I had before he was out. If he actually went out.

I prayed he went out. Lord, I prayed he went out.

Shit, what if I hadn't used enough? I hoped it would work, because there was no way I was actually going to go through with having sex with him. *Ew.* I'd find some way to bail before I did that.

When we got to the bed, I boldly pushed him back to sit on the edge of the mattress. Inside, I was praying like a priest on Sunday morning for the drugs to take effect.

"Damn, baby, I didn't know you were this feisty." His eyes registered mild shock at my behavior, but he grinned broadly, nonetheless.

"Lie down," I whispered as I leaned in and ran my nose along his neck. At least he smelled good, though he did absolutely zilch for me. Thankfully, he kicked off his shoes and did as I said. He propped his head on his hands as he continued to grin.

"I'm all yours," he said as he raised his hips suggestively.

God, no. Ugh.

Trying to hide the tremor of my hands, I unbuckled his belt and made a production of pulling it free from his pants. Taking my time, I unbuttoned his shirt slowly. I bit my lip and gave him what I hoped was a teasingly seductive glance.

Oh, sweet Jesus, give me strength.

Well then. While he was tall and lean, he obviously didn't take care of himself as well as Luke did. His stomach was a little paunchy when it wasn't disguised by his jacket and shirt.

Right when I was ever so slowly sliding his open shirt off his chest, he grabbed me and flipped us over so fast, I lost my breath.

"What are you doing?" I gasped. He was suddenly like a fucking octopus. Hands everywhere at once, tugging my dress up, raining kisses over my neck and chest. Panic started to well in me as I tried to stop him.

"Sorry, baby. I don't do submissive well." He nipped my neck, and I jerked my shoulder up to get him away.

Not the plan! Not the plan! Not the plan! Abort! Abort!

"Wait. Slow down," I breathlessly demanded. "I-I-I wanted us to take our time," I stuttered.

"Next time. I need you too bad right now. You tempting me in this tight, sexy dress all night drove me crazy. Like I wouldn't know you were flashing those pretty tits at me on purpose," he panted, and his wet lips trailed over my skin. I was beginning to worry I would be covered in his saliva by the end of it.

Eeeewww! I tried to wiggle away and remove his hands.

"But—" was all I got out before he kissed me. Then I gagged when he shoved his tongue down my throat. He didn't seem to notice as he moved back to my chest and bit my damn boob!

"Ow!" I reflexively smacked his head.

"Sorry, I can barely control myself around you," he apologized without really stopping.

Sweat broke out all over me. I had to keep telling myself I could do this. Simply needed to wait out the effects. Stall.

Jesus fucking Christ, why isn't that shit working?

I began to question whether I'd been duped. After all, I wasn't super savvy on buying illegal products. What if I'd been sold placebos or powdered sugar or something? Justine had gone out on a limb to get it for me. She'd be fired if anyone found out.

That's when I realized he was moving slower. He had pressed his face into my neck, and he attempted to bite me again, but he barely made contact before all of his weight went dead on me.

"Oh God," I wheezed. He was so heavy; I could barely get my lungs to expand. It took everything I had to get him wiggled off me. Glancing over at him, out of breath from my workout, I saw him staring at me as he lay prone in the bed, face turned my direction. "Chet?"

I waved my hand in front of his face, but he stared unblinkingly. I shook him, but he still didn't move.

Praying I hadn't used too much and killed him, I rested my ear against his back. The sound of his lungs filling with air had me exhaling in relief. His eyes being open creeped me out, but it was necessary for a minute.

I shoved my hands under him to get in the pockets of his slacks for his phone. It wasn't in the first one, nor was it in the next. "Shit!"

Scrambling off the bed, I ran to the kitchen and found his jacket hanging over one of the chair backs. In the inside pocket, I found what I was looking for. I rushed back to the bedroom and held the phone in front of his face, then checked. It worked!

"Thanks, Chet," I whispered before I reached over and closed his eyes. As quickly as I could, I went through his text messages. Nothing. Next, I checked his social media chats. Still nothing.

Flipping from screen to screen, I worried that maybe he messaged on his computer or something.

Dammit, I suck at this!

Then I spotted the "misc." folder and opened it to find a messenger app. It was password protected.

"Dammit! Please let it be facial recognition too," I whispered as I held it in front of his face and held his eyes wide with one hand.

The app popped open, and I tried to still my racing heart. I could not believe that worked.

At first, I was confused. There were only a few messages from today, and they all were from the same number. I could only assume he had deleted everything prior.

I rummaged around in his dresser and bedside drawers. I checked the closet, the spare bedrooms, the kitchen, everywhere—no other phone. "Maybe it's a partner," I whispered. The kids had said it was always him, though.

"Fuck, fuck, fuck! Think!" I tapped the phone against my thigh. Then I froze. Heart beating so hard I thought it would explode, I called the number in the messages.

It went to a voicemail that wasn't set up. That was when I realized I'd heard vibrating. I called it again. The vibrating commenced. Trying to hold myself still and barely breathing, I tried to locate it. Three calls later, I found it under the bed. There was a small slit cut in the box spring liner. The phone was in a baggie taped to the inside.

"Holy shit!" I whispered as I lay with my torso under the bed. "What the fuck do I do now?" It was one of those cheap store phones. No facial recognition; this had a passcode. I tried the last four digits of his actual phone number. Nothing. His house number. Nope.

The bed shifted above me, and I froze. Eyes wide, I held my breath. Looking at the time, I realized I'd been here longer than I'd planned. I had no idea how long he would actually be out. It wasn't every day I drugged people.

When no further sound ensued, I cautiously scooted out from under the bed and slowly rose up to peek over the edge. Eyes still closed, he had moved his arm and leg a bit.

Having no clue what to do next, I erased the calls I'd made from his phone, wiped it down with a dish towel, then used the towel to drop it back in his jacket. I grabbed my shoes and purse and tiptoed toward the door.

The story of the tell-tale heart came to mind, as every little sound seemed amplified. I caught a glimpse of myself in a mirror in the foyer and cringed. I looked awful. Closing the door as quietly as I could, I speed walked to the sidewalk and hopped on one foot as I slipped on one shoe, then the next.

My plan was to go a few blocks over, then call a cab.

Except a truck pulled up next to me, brakes screeching as it stopped, and I shrieked.

"Get in."

Chapter SIXTEEN

Snow

"DYING"—STONE SOUR

RAGE DIDN'T BEGIN TO TOUCH WHAT I WAS FEELING. SEEING her on a fucking date with that fucking prick Edwards pissed me off. Following them to his house after dropping off my mom was likely crazy and stupid, because it had me burning mad. Seeing her stumbling out of his house looking just-been-fucked had me ready to kill someone with my bare hands.

"I said, get the fuck in the truck, Hailey," I growled out through clenched teeth. She stood on the sidewalk staring wide-eyed and wild like a deer caught in my headlights. "Now!"

She jumped, and I momentarily regretted snapping at her.

She glanced around before she cautiously opened the door. Without a word, she climbed in and closed the door.

"Seat belt," I demanded.

Her hands shook as she did as I said. Hitting the gas, I rolled up the window as we roared out of the neighborhood. I didn't trust myself to say anything further.

With the rumble of the motor as the only thing breaking the silence, I drove back to my house. Fury burned like flames through my veins with every second that ticked by.

"Are you going to talk to me?" she finally whispered, obviously unable to stand the utter quiet.

Still not trusting myself not to scream at her, I clenched my jaw and kept my eyes on the road. She didn't speak until I pulled into my driveway and shut off my truck.

"I messed up," she murmured with a tremble in her voice. In the stillness of the cab, I could hear her swallow.

Unable to hold it in any longer, I turned to face her. "You think?" I shouted in incredulous disbelief.

Tears trailed down her cheeks, and some of the fire dimmed within me. I rested my elbows on the steering wheel and scrubbed my face with my hands. Taking measured breaths, I worked to calm myself as best I could before I said or did something I would regret.

"Let's go inside. You can shower, and I'll get you something clean to put on." It took everything in me not to look at how her dress was all stretched out and one of her tits was half exposed. Thank fuck she had a bra on, or I might not have been able to hold it in anymore.

When I got down from the truck, I slammed my door. She

still sat in the passenger seat, so I opened her door. "Did you lose your hearing? Let's go inside."

No matter how mad I was, I was glad I was standing there, because she literally fell out of the truck. "Jesus," I muttered. The thought began to settle in my head that Chet had hurt her, which set my anger in motion for a completely different reason.

A sob escaped her, and I huffed out a labored exhale before I wrapped her in my arms. When she settled into shuddering sniffles, I scooped her up and carried her to the house. She had her purse and hands clutched tight to her chest, but her face burrowed into my neck.

"I've got you," I sighed, not wanting to let her go again.

I carried her all the way to the master bath before I gently set her on her feet. The fury within was at a low simmer by then—not gone, but not raging. Firmly but gently, I took her purse and her phone and set them on the counter.

Head bowed, she stood there with her hair a tangled curtain over her face.

Like I was undressing a child, I slipped the dress and undergarments off her, feeling my teeth grinding at the scruff burns on her pale flesh. When I saw teeth marks on the top of her breast, I almost punched a hole in the wall.

"Hailey?"

She glanced at me briefly but didn't reply. The bold woman I knew was a mere shadow of herself.

"Hailey. Did he—" I swallowed with difficulty before I tried again, "Did he hurt you? Assault you?"

If he had, I would kill him with my bare hands. Tonight.

She shook her head, wide-eyed and shaken. A small sliver of relief hit me.

"Are you sure?"

She nodded before she whispered, "He thought I wanted to, but I didn't, I mean, I...."

Whipping the handle to hot, I started the shower. "Get in," I ordered her again. It took me propelling her in before she moved.

She jumped when the hot water hit her, and I adjusted the temperature. When she made no attempt to wash herself, I huffed in frustration and stripped down to my boxers before climbing in after her.

"Tip your head back."

She did as I said, and I wet her hair, then lathered a generous amount of shampoo in it. "Rinse." If I gave her exact commands, she obeyed. Thankfully I had conditioner that I used in my beard or I'd probably never get the tangles out of her hair.

Once she was clean, I shut off the water, dried her off, and carried her to my bed. Unable to stop myself, I pressed a kiss to her temple. Then I went in search of the hairbrush I remembered seeing in the spare bathroom. My mother had left it after she'd spent the night at my house last Christmas.

I stripped out of the wet underwear, gave myself a cursory dry, then pulled on some sleeping pants. After I was done, I returned to the bed where she still sat staring at the wall. I went through my drawers and found an old T-shirt and a pair of basketball shorts. My sleeping pants would be way too long for her, despite her height.

"Here," I said as I held the clothes out. When she stared at them but didn't move, I sighed and helped her dress.

Working through my words to prevent my thoughts from coming out the wrong way, I brushed her hair. Finally, when I had it smoothed, I set the brush on the nightstand. Needing space, I scooted back to lean against the headboard and rested my arms on my raised knees.

Though I hated to ask, I needed to know. It would decide whether I killed him immediately or dragged it out over time.

"What exactly did he do to you?"

She startled at my voice, but I remained calm and patient. Wide, scared eyes met mine before she shook her head.

"No what?"

She swallowed with difficulty. Then she croaked out, "He didn't do anything. I mean, not really. It's what I did."

"What?" My brow furrowed in confusion.

Blinking her eyes rapidly, she swallowed again. "Can I trust you?"

"What the fuck kind of question is that?" It probably came out harsher than I intended, because she flinched. Trying to regain my calm, I closed my eyes and breathed deeply. "Yes, you can absolutely trust me. I would lay down my life for you."

The words shocked her as much as they shocked me. We sat there unblinking for a moment before she whispered, "I drugged him."

"Come again?"

"I gave him Rohypnol," she clarified, and my eyes bugged.

"What the actual fuck? Where the fuck did you get that? It's illegal as fuck! And why the hell would you go out on a date with that fucker and then drug him?" My voice got louder with each word. There was nothing I truly feared, at least not until that moment. Something happening to her was clearly my worst nightmare.

Her bottom lip quivered, and I immediately felt like an ass.

"Why would you care?" she mumbled so softly, I barely heard her.

"Because you're *mine*, goddamn it!" I roared. At that, the tears fell rapidly.

Shit.

Contrite, I pulled her into my lap. She buried her face into my neck, and I cradled her head with my hand. My eyes fell shut as I kissed her forehead.

"He's getting kids hooked on drugs and prostituting them," she sobbed in a watery blubbering mess.

Shock hit me as I fought to process her tearful words. How the fuck did I not know this was going on in my area? Maybe she was mistaken. He was a dick, but fucking hell, he was a cop. In the back of my mind, a voice whispered that he'd done it before.

She seemed to calm down after crying it out a bit.

"Are you sure?"

"No. But that's what the kids told me. I went to get proof. I found his disposable phone, but it was locked. I was afraid the drugs would wear off and he would wake up, so I left." She sniffled. My heart stuttered, and my stomach bottomed out at the insane risk she'd taken. I closed my eyes and took a deep breath to prevent losing my shit. What the hell was she hoping to accomplish with her ridiculously dangerous stunt?

"Okay, where does he keep it? I can send someone in to retrieve it and try to hack it."

"I took it," she softly admitted, and my blood ran cold.

"Holy shit."

"Damn, he deleted shit, but thankfully I'm a badass. It's all still here. At least for the last month. Shithead in the dungeon must've been right; looks like he switches burners once a month." Hacker was tapping away at lightning speed on his laptop.

"Fuck." It was all I could say. We only had the last month, but it was something.

"What do you want to do with this?" Reaper asked. He was my new sergeant at arms since losing Lock and Gunny; I knew he was making mental preparations.

Once I'd found out what Hailey had done, I knew she'd painted a huge target on her back. Even if he didn't remember what happened last night, it wouldn't take a genius to put the pieces together when he realized his "business" phone was missing. At least we had something to go on, but if we didn't get to the bottom of this ASAP, Hailey would have a price on her head and never be safe.

Fucking hell.

"Goddamn it. I wish she'd come to me instead of trying to play secret agent. We need to find out how far this goes. If Chet Edwards works for some shithead higher up or if he's an opportunist piece of shit that works on his own." My hand raked through my hair. I had no issues hiring Venom's club to make Officer Chet Edwards disappear. Except, other than possibly keeping Hailey safe, it would be a pointless move if he was merely a cog.

"Well, we know he's getting his supply from somewhere, because he's not manufacturing the shit. And we know he's supplying kids to sickos, but we need to find out how he gets hooked up with those sick fucks," Soap inserted.

"I'm working on that too, but there's a reason people do that shit on the dark web. It's hard as hell to figure out where things originate. I'm good, but these people are just as good, and some are better," Hacker said with an irritated sigh.

Looking around the table, I took in the serious expressions on the faces of all of my brothers. No one would refuse to help with this, but I owed them the truth about why I was set on rescuing Hailey. By bringing her to our clubhouse, I'd brought her trouble to our doorstep.

Working my jaw, I dropped my gaze to the scarred tabletop, then met my brothers' eyes one by one. What I was about to announce was unprecedented for me and as such was difficult to admit.

No coward, I hardened my expression and lifted my chin. Daring anyone to question me, I finally said, "Hailey is mine."

Confusion marred their faces before several broke out in grins.

"Boss man, are you saying you're *claiming* a woman?" Hollywood asked with a stupid-ass smile splitting his face in two. I narrowed my eyes at him.

"Shut the fuck up," I grumbled. "I said it, didn't I?"

"Ho-ly shitballs," Cash murmured. Having been around since I was a prospect, he knew how out of character my declaration was.

"Moving on," I pointedly said. A few smothered chuckles made their way to me, and I sent out a glare.

"Like Soap said, we need to find out how deep Chet Edwards is in this shit. Find out if he's only selling the shit or, if what we uncovered on the phone is implying what we think it's implying, he's tied up in the mess with Danielle. I'm leaning toward that being the case, because I don't like how he showed up at Hailey's office to tell her about them finding her. It didn't sit right with me. It seemed like he was fishing to see if any of the kids had said anything." I leaned back in my chair.

"Well, the shit on his burner phone sure sounds like he was involved. I'll see what else I can find." Hacker closed his eyes and raked a hand through his hair.

"What the hell was her plan anyway?" Reaper asked. As I shook my head, I rolled my eyes.

"She didn't really have one. Well, not much of one," I muttered. "She thought she'd find out who he was working with and tell the authorities."

"Jesus, didn't she know that wouldn't be admissible?" Vinny questioned with bugging eyes. Though he had been relaxed in his seat, he quickly sat upright.

"Obviously she didn't think that through," I said as I dragged a hand down my face.

"No shit," Hollywood agreed with his astonished expression matching every other brother in the room.

"Any other questions?" I asked after a heavy sigh.

Silence filled the room.

I ended church, and we filed out. Hollywood beelined for his ol' lady. He, Reaper, and I were heading over to see Baker, but he only had a small window of time for us, so we needed to get on the road. Tash was in the common area talking to Hollywood's ol' lady, Becca, who Hollywood was now draped around as she laughed.

With a wave of my hand, I flagged Tash over. She broke away and approached me with a quizzical expression. "Yeah, Snow?"

"I need you to check on Hailey. She's in my room. I don't think she's eaten anything since yesterday. See if you can round something up for her in the kitchen."

"No problem," she said with a nervous smile.

"Thanks," I said to her before making a circle in the air with my finger and telling the boys, "Let's go!"

We were supposed to meet with Stuart's supplier tonight, but I had a feeling that wasn't going to happen. Considering we had a good idea of who it was and Hailey had taken his goddamn phone. I sighed in frustration.

Hollywood shoved his fingers into his wife's hair and kissed her goodbye. I debated going to check on Hailey myself, but we were on a time crunch and I was the goddamn president. I refused to look like a pussy.

So instead, I roared out of the lot, pipes crackling and my brothers at my back.

Chapter SEVENTEEN

Hailey

"STOP AND SAY YOU LOVE ME"—EVANS BLUE

A KNOCK ON THE DOOR WOKE ME, AND I SLEEPILY PUSHED UP in the bed. "Yeah?" I croaked.

Blonde hair streaked with hot pink piled in a messy bun was the first thing I saw, as a woman peeked in. "Hey," she said with a soft grin. "Snow asked me to come check on you. I brought you a sandwich and some chips."

My stomach dropped, and my chest ached at what this woman might be to him.

"Um, okay?" I didn't know what to say, because I was dying to ask her.

She brought in a bamboo tray and set it on the bedside table. Then she dropped into the desk chair and crossed long, tanned legs. Her shorts had barely covered her ass, and she had a loose-fitting off-the-shoulder shirt over a tank top. She looked perfectly sloppy in the sexiest of ways, and I instantly hated her.

My stomach rumbled.

"I made the sandwich plain 'cause I didn't know what you liked. There's some mayo and mustard packets on there. If you want me to get lettuce and tomato, I can. Oh, and I made some Chai tea and grabbed a bottle of water." She shrugged as she apologetically wrinkled her nose. It only made her more adorable, and I really despised her then. I'd be lying if I said I didn't want to claw her big blue eyes out.

"It's fine. Who are you?" I asked in an offhand tone. My gaze flicked up from where I doctored the sandwich to covertly look at her.

A knowing smirk lit her face, and I fought a growl. "I'm Tasha. You can call me Tash. I'm not with Snow and never have been," she said before she pulled her disgustingly plush lips between her teeth. That's when what she said registered and made me feel like an asshole.

"Oh." My face flamed as I shoved the food in my face. I'd had some awfully hateful thoughts about her that she hadn't deserved.

An awkward silence was broken only by the sound of my chewing. I'd gotten halfway through the meal when I stopped. Frozen stock-still, my hands began to shake, and my eyes went wide.

After nearly falling on my face, I gracelessly scrambled out of the bed. I bolted to the bathroom, where I proceeded to vomit up every bite I'd eaten. "Ugh," I moaned after the last round of dry heaves.

"Damn, I'm not the best cook, but I've never had that response to my sandwiches." Tash's voice came from the open doorway. Slowly, I rolled my head in her direction. My entire body was trembling.

"I'm sorry. I think it's all the stress," I muttered thickly before I carefully climbed up, using the wall for support. On shaking legs, I shuffled to the sink and cupped my hand in the running water to rinse the vile taste from my mouth. Spotting a tube of toothpaste, I put some on my finger and brushed my teeth as best as I could.

When I moved toward the door, Tash backed up, and I could see a calculating gleam in those pale blue eyes. It took a lot for me to make it back to the bed, even with her supporting me.

She tucked me in like a mother would as she chewed on her lip. "Have you been sick before this?"

"A couple times, but with everything that's happened lately, my nerves are shot."

"It's not my business, but, um, could you be pregnant?"

"Absolutely not."

"No chance at all?"

If I was honest, I couldn't say that for sure. Nervously, I tried to think of when I'd had my period last, but I drew a blank. It could've been last week, but I honestly couldn't think. Grimacing slightly, I shrugged.

She blew out a big breath. "Okay. Chill here for a second. 'Kay?"

Closing my eyes, I nodded.

Tash was gone a few minutes before she returned with a small box in her hands. "They say the best time to take one is first thing in the morning, but we can see what it says, then maybe do another one in the morning?"

"You got a stockpile of those?" I grumbled.

"Sort of." She shrugged but didn't meet my gaze. My heart went out to her if she was constantly having to check to see if she was pregnant. Didn't they make sure their club girls were on birth control? God, I hoped they used condoms. The stuff from that TV show flashed through my head, and my stomach churned a bit.

"Oh" was all I could say.

"I mean, they keep them in the infirmary, you know, just in case." Her cheeks flushed a rosy pink, which made her dusting of freckles stand out. She really was a pretty girl, and I wondered about her story. I really wanted to ask, but it seemed rude.

"You think I should use it now?" Suddenly, I wanted to cling to her like she was my best friend. I hated to admit I was terrified because Luke and I weren't *together,* together.

What if he thought I'd gotten pregnant on purpose to try to trap him? I huffed out in frustration as I threw the covers back again and traipsed back to the bathroom. It didn't matter. I'd deal with whatever the plastic stick said. If it was on my own, so be it. I'd been prepared to be a single mom anyway.

Fuck it.

I followed the instructions and waited.

Arms folded and foot tapping, I stared at it.

"It won't finish quicker just because you're glaring at it."

I threw a sidelong glance toward Tash as I pursed my lips with impatience.

Her phone started to beep.

"Did you set a timer?" I asked in surprise.

She chuckled. "Yeah, because I figured you didn't."

I shot her a half-assed glare and picked up the test. "Well, shit."

Her brows rose, and she wrinkled her nose as she bit her lip. I turned the results in her direction.

The little screen flashed "pregnant."

I'd been waiting all afternoon for Luke to return. I was antsy, irritated, and damn near climbing the walls. It had been less than twenty-four hours, and already, I had cabin fever from being stuck in their clubhouse.

Okay, sure, at home I might veg out in front of my fireplace with a good book for my entire weekend. The difference? I could leave if I wanted.

It took me 317 steps to make a lap of the building. Inside, that was, and in the areas I had access to. I'd walked the entire interior once before I started watching my steps on my watch. After having me call into work to tell them I had a family emergency back home, Luke had taken my phone. He'd essentially disassembled and destroyed it when I'd finished the call, so I couldn't call him to see where he was.

Tash had gone to work, or I'd have asked to borrow hers.

"You're making me nervous. Can't you sit still for five minutes?" the gruff older man asked.

"Cash, is it?" I asked after looking at his patch. He nodded. "Perhaps you could call Luke—I mean, Snow?"

I'd really wanted to tell him to go fuck himself but decided that might not be a good idea. The saying my mother had always used came to mind about catching more flies with honey than vinegar. He appeared to be hesitantly considering my request, so I gave him what I hoped was a pleading smile.

He cleared his throat before replying with, "Well, I can try, but he may not answer."

"Thank you," I said in my sweetest tone.

Except he'd barely put the phone to his ear when the sound of several motorcycles roared out front. He dropped it and stood. "Let me go make sure that's them."

He'd made it halfway to the door when it banged open and Luke stepped through followed by several of the other club members. My heart skittered wildly at the sight of him, and I inwardly groaned at myself.

Those dark blue eyes locked on me as he approached me without pause. When he wrapped his big hand around the back of my neck and pulled me into the hottest kiss of my life, I lost all sense of where we were.

My arms wrapped around him and under his cut. Like he was my lifeline, I dug my fingers tightly into the firm muscles of his back. If I could've, I'd have hopped up and gripped his hips with my legs.

Instead, he growled and did it for me. Without breaking our kiss, he carried me back to his room. After we entered, he kicked the door shut behind him and climbed on the bed with me.

"I need you," he growled into my neck after he broke free and gasped for air. My back arched in need, all thoughts of what I needed to tell him simply gone.

"Yes," I moaned as he nipped down my neck, shoved my shirt up, and sucked on the swell of my breast. I tugged at his hair—trying desperately to pull him closer.

When he suddenly reared back and raked his teeth over his bottom lip, I gasped. The heat in his gaze was smoldering. "Get naked."

Usually, being told what to do would piss me off. Except with him, when we fucked, I loved his take-charge attitude. With everything that had happened lately, I needed to let go and have someone else make the decisions—at least for the moment.

In short order, I peeled my clothes off before I reached with greedy hands to help him get the rest of his removed. There would be time for talking afterward.

"I can't get enough of you," he whispered into my shoulder before he nipped the flesh and soothed it with his tongue. Soft moans escaped me as he followed an invisible map on my body.

With each touch and stroke of his fingers, I found myself wanting more. More of his touch, more of him, more than the arrangement we had. I began to panic at the thought. I'd sworn not to develop feelings, but I'd messed up. He'd become far too important to me.

There was the very real possibility that he was going to be furious with me when I told him I was pregnant, so I decided to enjoy this last scrap of him I might have.

"I need you," I whimpered as I studied every carved inch of his body. He was in his prime and absolutely gorgeous in a rugged, bad-boy way. It was obvious he kept himself in shape, and I appreciated that more than he knew.

Trailing my tongue along my lower lip, I raised my hands

to the headboard and grasped it tightly. Fire burned in his gaze, molten and consuming. He nudged my legs further apart with his knees as he sheathed his length. For a brief moment, maniacal laughter wanted to bubble up as I fought the urge to tell him there was no need.

Testing how ready I was, he dipped into my entrance several times, each stroke slightly deeper than the last until finally he was fully seated within me. The sensations he evoked were unparalleled. The slow, sensual movements as he held my gaze made my heart sing a foolish melody.

The sound of our ragged breaths and the wet slide of our connected bodies filled the room. Not once did his eyes leave mine. Wanting more, I wrapped my legs around his and urged him toward me.

With a growl, he pulled out, flipped me over until I rested on my hands and knees, and plunged deep again. I gasped and looked over my shoulder. His fingers were splayed and digging into my ass and hips as he started to move. He watched his cock slip in and out of me with parted lips, a heated gaze, and soft grunts each time he bottomed out.

My head dropped as his thumb joined his shaft briefly, then circled the pucker of my ass. A whimper escaped me when he pushed past the tight ring, and I tensed.

"Relax," he whispered before leaning forward to run kisses up my back to my shoulder. The featherlight touch of his lips and soft beard sent shivers skating across my skin. Each time he buried himself in my pussy, he slid his thumb in a little more. The forbidden aspect of it seemed to intensify everything I was experiencing.

There were no words to describe how I was feeling. In fact, I could barely form a coherent thought.

Unbidden, tears welled in my eyes before spilling over on the pillow below me. Not from pain, but from an overabundance of emotion. Steady and sure, he continued to stroke. His other hand reached around to circle my clit, and I groaned low and feral.

Before I knew it, the pressure of my pending orgasm burst, and nothing registered except the clenching of my core around his thick cock. White sparks exploded behind my clenched lids, and a mewled litany slipped from my lips.

"Yessss… there… uhhhhh!"

He rode out my climax until my arms collapsed and my face fell to the bed. Eyes closed, I sensed him leaning over me before the bed dipped on either side of me where his arms held him up. He nuzzled my hair to the side to reach the sensitive spot on my neck.

"I've missed the feel of this pussy squeezing my cock," he breathlessly whispered. I wanted to cry at his words because they only emphasized the differences in where our heads were.

I'd missed more than the sex. I'd missed *him*.

His smile.

His deep laughter.

His ability to know my every need before I did.

The way his eyes crinkled in the corners when he grinned.

The way he absently stroked his beard when he was deep in thought.

"Baby?" he asked, pulling me from my musings. "You good?"

I nodded into the linens, and he lifted, leaving me chilled. His grip on me tightened, and he gave a quick snap of his hips.

A surprised gasp was forced out of me at how good he was at what he did. Not allowing me any time to recuperate, he began thrusting at a rapid pace.

"Yes," I murmured. "So good."

Relentless, he fucked me until I was screaming his name. Then he wrapped my hair around his hand as he growled. He arched my back with a tug on my tresses as his rhythm faltered.

The clenching spasms between my legs hit at the same time as he sank his teeth into my shoulder. A guttural sound was followed by his animalistic roar as he released my flesh from his bite. He continued to pound into me as his cock pulsed, filling the condom.

Spent, he gently laid me down and curled his warm body around mine. Gentle kisses soothed where he'd left his mark. For a moment we quietly calmed our breathing. The absolute rightness of the way he remained sheathed in my core as he held me had me yearning for that something more again.

"Luke, I can't do this anymore," I finally whispered when I found my voice.

The instant tensing of his frame behind me preceded the separation of our bodies. It left me desolate and aching.

Though I tried to fight him, he firmly turned me to my back. I closed my eyes tightly to avoid allowing him to read more than I wanted. His hand gently squeezed my jaw.

"Open your eyes and look at me." The demand was growled, not spoken, but I was afraid.

Afraid he'd read my thoughts like a book if I let him actually see me.

"Hailey. What the fuck are you saying?"

Was that hurt I heard in the crack of his voice? Worry? Or was I hearing emotions that weren't there?

"Goddamn it. Be a grown-up and look. At. Me."

After gathering every scrap of strength I could, I slowly lifted my lids. His brows knit as he searched my face.

Telling myself I needed to stick to my guns and disengage before it was too late, I blinked rapidly. It was time to walk away before I completely lost my heart to a man who wouldn't give me his in return.

The best I could, I hardened my emotions. Except his next words blew me away and sent my hackles up at the same time.

"Hailey, you're mine. You feel me?"

Again, I blinked owlishly. Then I sputtered.

"What? You don't own me, you know. I'm not a lump of meat that you can fight over or claim." As I scowled, he barked out a laugh.

"A lump of meat?" He chuckled.

"It's not funny." I fumed as he continued to chuckle and nuzzled into my cleavage.

Though I tried to be firm, his beard tickled my chest, and I wiggled under him as I snickered softly. Of course, that only made him do it more.

When I couldn't stand it any longer, I gripped his hair tightly and pulled him back. I was gasping for breath as he grinned with a twinkle in his eye.

"What exactly are *you* saying?" I breathlessly whispered.

"I'm saying that I did something I've never in my life done."

"Which is?"

"Claimed a woman to my brothers."

Chapter EIGHTEEN

Snow

"FIRST TIME"—FINGER ELEVEN

THE EXPRESSION ON HER FACE TOLD ME THAT SHE DIDN'T understand the significance of what I had said.

Realizing I needed to explain, I rolled out of the bed, disposed of the well-used condom, and strode back to the bed. The entire time, I could feel, then see her eyes following my every move.

Unashamed of my nudity, I sat next to her.

"So you're saying you pissed on me? Metaphorically speaking?" she asked, eyes comically wide.

Her question made me laugh. "No. But they know you're

mine and they will do everything in their power to ensure your safety, just as I would do the same for one of their ol' ladies or family members."

At the term "ol' ladies," her nose wrinkled. I leaned down to kiss the tip of it as I grinned.

"Don't call me old," she grumbled.

"It's actually a term of endearment," I said, and she snorted in disbelief. "It's true," I argued. Her expression told me she still didn't buy it, but I'd have Steph, Kassi, and Sera talk to her to explain it better than I could.

"I know that, but I don't like it," she muttered.

I chuckled.

"Where did you go today?" She gave me a belligerent scowl. I sighed.

"Club business," I evasively replied. There was no way I'd tell her we broke back into Chet's house and returned the phone to where she'd described it being. He might know it had been messed with, but hopefully, he hadn't checked yet. We also thoroughly searched the house and planted a few listening devices.

If it was the last thing I did, I was going to nail his ass for the shit he'd been doing. After talking with Venom, I also found out he was one of the cops who'd given his ol' lady, Loralei, a bunch of shit while she was here.

Fucking asshole.

"Hmpf!" she huffed as she rolled her eyes.

"Look, I'm not trying to be a dick, but there are some things that are better you don't know." She appeared to be mulling over what I'd said as she picked at nonexistent lint on the covers she'd slipped under.

When she didn't say anything, I joined her under the bed linens and gathered her close. Her head lay on my chest, leg twined with mine, and her hand rested over my pounding heart. This was extremely difficult for me, and I was tempted to let it lie, but I couldn't. What I'd admitted to her was huge.

As I spoke, I sifted her silken honey-colored hair through my fingers.

"You've told me you're not old, you've griped about me marking my territory, and you've been pissed at me for being gone today, but you haven't actually addressed what I told you. I know what I said when we started our arrangement, but somewhere along the line, things changed. The joke was definitely on me when we made that agreement, because I had no idea how easily you'd get under my skin. The thought of you being with anyone else makes me feel like my heart is rotting inside my chest. I'll never force you to stay with me if you don't feel the same, but I want you in more than my bed—I want you in my life. You mean something to me. I—You somehow found a way to make me love you," I ended in an amazed whisper. I'd poured my heart out like a fucking pussy, but it needed to be said. With bated breath, I waited for her to say something.

She inhaled deeply and let out a shuddering exhale. Her fingers clutched me like she never wanted to let me go. Right when I thought she had chickened out or I was a fool, she dropped a bomb on me that changed everything.

"I'm pregnant," she whispered.

If the world had split in two and I'd fallen through, I couldn't have been more stunned.

And devastated.

Fighting to breathe, I moved her off me and sat on the edge of the bed. Betrayal ripped through me, and pain like nothing I'd experienced ravaged me.

"Luke?" she whispered, oblivious to the fact that she'd ruined us with her statement.

As stoically as I could when my rib cage was in a vise and I couldn't expand my lungs to breathe, I stood. Afraid to look at her in case I weakened, I said over my shoulder, "Nice try, honey, but it ain't mine. I've had a vasectomy."

Forcing one foot in front of the other, I went to the bathroom doorway.

"Luke!" Her strangled shout snapped through me like a bullet. I flinched when her hand curled around my bicep. She ducked under my arm, wrapped in the sheet, holding it by one hand.

"I'll get you moved to the guest room. I won't turn you out, but you can't stay in here." Through each word, I refused to meet her silver gaze. If I did, I might crack. I'd let her have such power over me that I was tempted to tell her it didn't matter if she'd cheated or was lying to me.

"Goddamn it, Luke! Now who's being childish? Look at me!" she demanded, but I stubbornly refused. "My name isn't *honey*, and we also used condoms. Considering you're the only motherfucker I've slept with in the last two years, we have a problem. Either your procedure didn't work or it was the immaculate conception of the second coming, which I doubt. Regardless, it sure as hell is yours!"

Roughly, I dragged a hand through my hair and then down my face. My heart wanted to believe her so fucking bad. A small voice in the back of my head said that she wasn't deceitful, but I couldn't wrap my head around it.

I needed some time.

Gently, I moved her out of the way, then closed the bathroom door and locked it. She pounded on the other side as she yelled my name. I bowed my head and leaned it on the wood. Gutted didn't begin to describe how I was feeling.

I hadn't lied. I loved her. Heart and soul. But she'd sliced me open in one fell swoop, and I was reeling.

Silence fell as she quit beating on the door. Unable to stand the smell of her on me because it was making me want to crawl back out there and tell her it didn't matter, I still loved her, I got in the shower. The water hadn't heated yet, and I sucked in a startled breath as the cold hit me.

The water had gotten hot, then cold again, before the pounding started once more.

"Stop!" I roared.

The pounding ended, but it was Reaper's voice I heard call out through the wood. "Prez, you need to come out here."

Defeat heavy in my heart, I stepped out of the shower and wrapped a towel low on my hips. When I swung the door open, Reaper's worried gaze hit mine.

"What?" I demanded. His next words shouldn't have had such a profound effect, but they further destroyed me.

"Hailey left."

Goddamn it.

Chapter
NINETEEN

Hailey

"THE HUNTED"—SAINT ASONIA (FEAT. SULLY ERNA)

Disbelief initially held me frozen outside the locked bathroom door. I'd stood there staring at the marred wood feeling like my entire world was crumbling. I kept telling myself I was in a nightmare and willed myself to wake up.

When I heard the water start in the bathroom, I knew he was ignoring me.

After stumbling on the sheet that dragged behind me, I'd caught myself on the edge of the mattress. Tears streamed down my cheeks, and a sob broke loose.

I blindly pulled on clothes and shoved the few things Luke and I had packed the night before into my small tote.

Had it really only been twenty-four hours since I'd climbed in his truck? Twenty-four hours since I'd tried to play detective? Unreal.

"I'm not crazy," I whispered to myself as I shoved shoes on my feet and wiped away my tears. "I haven't been with anyone but him."

Head bowed, I left the room without a backward glance. I'd made it down the hall and through the main area of the clubhouse before I'd seen anyone. When one of them had called out, I'd given a wave but essentially ignored them and kept moving.

I'd gotten lucky when I went outside. There was someone in a truck parked at the entrance to the clubhouse. The driver was laughing and talking with the guy manning the gate, allowing me to slip through the dark shadows of the building to where Luke had one of his guys park my vehicle.

Sitting in the dark interior, I debated what my next move should be.

"Doesn't matter. I'll figure it out as I go," I said before I briefly rested my forehead on the steering wheel. Gathering every bit of fortitude I had, I breathed deep and exhaled slowly.

As I started my car, I fought crying again. No one had come after me, but I didn't expect it. I followed the truck out of the gate with a friendly wave to the guy standing there. The truck went right; I went left.

"There's no way he had a vasectomy. What a crock of shit! The nerve of him. If he didn't want to step up and be a father, he should've just said so," I muttered nonstop as I drove toward town. "Fuck him and the horse he rode in on."

When I got to my house, I quickly packed a suitcase, dragged it out to my car, and heaved it into the trunk. It had been less than thirty minutes since I'd left Luke behind. Despite his behavior, I already missed him.

Since I already called in to work at Luke's urging, I figured I might as well head to my parents. At least until I could come up with a plan. What sucked was that I had to hide from Chet even though I didn't actually have any proof against him. Yet thanks to my irrational decision to leave Chet's house with that damn phone, he would be gunning for me. Luke was right about that.

I'd almost made it out of town when flashing lights lit up my rearview, and my heart went into overdrive.

"Shit!" I reluctantly pulled over, thankful that Chet worked days. Still, my heart slammed against my rib cage and my hands shook. My grip on the wheel tightened to steady them.

As the officer approached my car, I rolled down my window.

"Step out of the car," the officer said, shining a light in my face. My eyes rebelled against the blinding light, and my stomach bottomed out at the recognition of his voice. I debated slamming it in drive and taking off.

"Don't do it," Officer Chet Edwards said, reading my mind. My breath caught, and it was like I was suffocating.

He pulled my door open and motioned for me to get out with the barrel of his gun.

"It wasn't a request, Hailey. Get your ass out of the car. Right fucking now or things will get really ugly for a lot of people."

"Chet, I wasn't even going that fast," I said when I stood in front of him, trying to play things off. Maybe he hadn't discovered the phone missing. It was possible. Maybe.

"Let's not play stupid. We both know what the deal is. Shut your car off and let's go."

My mind was racing, trying to think of a way I could leave a clue or call for help. Except I was coming up blank. Luke had destroyed my phone to prevent Chet from tracking me, and I hadn't thought I'd need another one so soon. It wasn't like I had a lot of options.

Stopping by my back tire, he pulled out a knife and shoved it in between the treads.

"Get moving," he demanded, and I reluctantly shuffled to his cruiser. He opened the back door and motioned for me to get in. Panic clawed at my throat, choking me. Who knew how long it would be before someone found my car or reported me missing? No one would be expecting me at work. Luke thought I was a liar.

Justine was the only one who might miss me, but only if she didn't call my office and find out I was "home on a family emergency."

The slamming of the door once I was inside was symbolic of my coffin closing. The thought of my life ending, and that of my little bean that I'd barely had time to wrap my head around—too much.

Unable to stop myself, I started to quietly cry. After silence for several miles, I finally couldn't stand it. "What are you going to do with me?"

"It wasn't supposed to go like this. That stupid club was supposed to take the fall for it after we planted Danielle's clothing in their clubhouse! Then you had to fuck it up," he muttered. "Why the fuck couldn't you leave well enough alone?"

"I was supposed to let you continue to exploit the kids in the program?" I asked in absolute disbelief at his thought process and the fact that he had framed Luke's club.

"None of those kids mattered! I made sure to only take the ones that wouldn't be missed!" he screamed at me like an utter madman. The Chet of my date and of the local police was visible nowhere in this wide-eyed, spittle-spewing madman.

Astonished that he could say that or believe it, I was momentarily speechless.

"Chet… they were children. Children who were trying to get their lives back together. What difference does it make if they 'wouldn't be missed,' as you put it? No one deserves to be bought and sold like cattle."

His eyes met mine in the rearview mirror. "This is bigger than you have any clue about. You had to go sticking your nose into shit that didn't pertain to you. Now you've forced my hand. You won't bring as much, but you'll be out of my hair, and turning you over might keep them off my ass."

"What are you talking about?" I demanded.

"I can't have your body turn up around here. So you're just going to disappear."

My blood ran cold.

Chapter TWENTY

Snow

"HEAR ME NOW"—BAD WOLVES (FEAT. DIAMANTE)

I'D SENT SEVERAL OF THE GUYS OUT TO LOOK FOR HAILEY WHILE I headed to her house in the SUV. Despite the shit she'd tried to pull, the thought of something happening to her because she made a reckless decision to leave didn't sit well.

Except she wasn't there.

Since I had her garage code, I'd gone in to check her house. It was evident she'd been there, because her room was a mess of clothes tossed on the bed. None of which were there when I'd helped her pack a small bag to go to the clubhouse.

I called her best friend, Justine. "Hey, Justine. Have you seen Hailey?"

"No, I haven't. Why?" she suspiciously questioned.

"No specific reason. We've been playing phone tag," I smoothly lied. "I figured I'd just go to her instead of trying to reach her on the phone." If she didn't know where Hailey was, then who would?

Unsure of where to go next since Hollywood, Reaper, and Blue had all checked in saying she wasn't at any of the places they'd scoped out, I stared at my phone. Needing to talk to someone in a way I couldn't with my own brothers, I hit Venom's contact image.

It rang twice before he answered. "Snow?"

"Venom."

He chuckled. "We doing this again?"

I shook my head and snorted a humorless laugh. Then I filled him in on the shitstorm my life had become. He quietly listened until I'd spilled almost everything.

"She told me she's pregnant and it's mine," I finally admitted as I ducked my head and massaged my temples. Saying it out loud set my teeth on edge and sent a shaft of pain through my chest.

"Ohhh, damn," Venom replied.

"Yeah. So you know what that means. You know that's impossible," I muttered. "It means she lied to me and she was fucking someone else."

Then he shocked me by laughing. I'm not talking about a brief chuckle, this was full-on uproarious laughter.

"What the hell is so funny? I don't think anything about this is motherfuckin' funny." Anger bloomed in my chest.

167

"Chill, bro. I'm laughing because, come on… you can't be that dumb. You had that shit done in fucking Mexico, bro. When the Army docs refused to do the ol' snip-snip on you because of your age and the fact that you had no kids, you had me and Smoke take you across the border. We were drunk as hell." He laughed again. "Oh, this is priceless."

"We weren't *that* drunk," I muttered.

"Bullshit. The fact that we didn't kill ourselves, or someone else, driving there was a miracle. Holy shit, that was a night. Christ, I thought you were going to lose your goddamn cock and balls from that stunt. That place was sketchy as fuck. That you still have a functioning dick is more shocking than the possibility of you knocking someone up. That hack didn't know what the fuck he was doing." Venom was cracking up. Though he was seeing humor in the situation, I was beginning to feel slightly ill.

"Bro, that was a long time ago. You mean to tell me that in almost twenty years she's the only one I've knocked up?" I was trying to rationalize the situation to assuage the guilt that was beginning to come to the surface. I'd been an asshole to Hailey because I was convinced I couldn't get her pregnant.

"Hey. I don't claim to know the ways of the universe. I just know that everything happens for a reason. Trust me on that one, bro. If you want, I can have Voodoo talk to you," he offered.

A chill shot down my spine. Voodoo was a great guy, but something about him always put me on edge. Having the gift he did was slightly unnerving.

"I don't know. Maybe." I shrugged, though he couldn't see me. I finished filling him in on her running off and us not being able to find her yet.

"I'll call you back," he said and ended the call before I could reply.

"Fuck!" I shouted into the quiet of the SUV. Could I have been that wrong? I mean, yeah, the doc in Mexico was sketchy, but I'd never had a single chick accuse me of getting her pregnant in nearly twenty years.

Why would I have any reason to question that it hadn't been a successful procedure?

My phone rang, and I thought it was Venom calling me back already, so I didn't look at the display. "That was quick."

"Huh?" It wasn't Venom.

"Baker?"

"Yeah. We've got trouble. I was on duty tonight because Nelson called in sick. I had a speed trap set up on the edge of the city limit. Saw fucking Edwards pull over that chick you're banging and put her in his car. I just started following them with my fucking lights out. I'm calling you before I call it in." His words sent both relief and dread pouring through me.

"Where are you?"

He gave me his location, and I told him to stay on them. Then I called the boys and filled them in.

"Fucking Edwards has gone off the deep end," Reaper said as I drove toward the location. "Do not go in without us. You hear me?"

"Yeah, sure." I was lying through my teeth. No way was I waiting for anyone. This ended tonight.

"Snow!" Reaper shouted through the phone as I ended the call and hauled ass in the direction Baker was headed.

When I got close, I called Baker back.

"You call this in?" I asked him, needing to know what my options were.

"No, but I'm going to have to if I keep tailing them. You want me to handle this or do you want to deal with it?" Baker knew he was crossing a line by not calling it in, but our long-standing friendship trumped everything, and for that I was grateful.

"Where are you now? Any changes?" I asked. He filled me in on his current location and direction of travel.

"I'll be there in less than five minutes," I said.

"Roger that," he replied as I rounded the bend in the road that skirted the lake. Ahead, I saw headlights and taillights breaking through the pitch-black night. "Is that you coming up?"

"Yep. Pull off to the side, and I'll keep going. With any luck, he'll think I'm just a random traveler coming up behind him. And Baker?"

"Yeah?"

"I owe you one," I admitted. He snorted in disagreement.

"Dude, whatever. Like I said before, you've helped me on more occasions than I could count. I'm not worried about it, but try not to leave me a mess to explain or clean up," he replied with a heavy sigh.

"I got you," I assured him as I passed his cruiser on the side of the road. We ended our call, and I made note of the turn-off Edwards took as I went past. Once I was sure he'd gone far enough up the drive, I whipped a U-turn and killed my lights as I coasted to the side of the road before the driveway he'd taken.

I checked my weapons, sent my location to the boys, and went in on foot. They could be pissed at me all they wanted.

The driveway was bordered on either side by tall trees and

curved back and forth as it seemed to go on forever. In the back of my mind, the place seemed familiar, but I couldn't place it in the dark.

Once I reached the clearing at the end of the drive, I realized why I knew the location. It was the old bible camp. When we were kids, everyone used to go stay there for a couple of weeks every summer.

It had been owned by Edwards's parents and run in conjunction with their church. I'd forgotten about it after I left for the Army. I didn't know they still owned it before they died. Then again, it had been years.

My phone vibrated, and I stepped back in the deep shadows of the trees.

"You got my location I sent you?" I whispered as I kept my attention on my surroundings.

"Yeah, but what happened to you not going in alone?" Hacker demanded. I snorted softly.

"I don't have time for a lecture," I quietly argued.

"Yeah, well, you might like to know that ol' Chet likely killed his parents off for their money and that property you're on right now," Hacker said.

"What? I thought they died in a boating accident?"

"They did, but the details never sat well with the sheriff's department. No one could prove it wasn't an accident, despite the fact that the boat was brand-new and they were proficient boaters. It was too convenient, but the proof was lacking," Hacker explained.

"Look, we can discuss this later. I need to get up to the house before he hurts her. See you soon." Hailey and her impulsive ass needed me.

As I ended the call, I heard Hacker cursing. I turned my phone to silent and shoved it back in my pocket.

Staying along the tree line, I mapped out the lay of the place. The old lake home had seen better days. The cabins the kids stayed in weren't in much better shape. There was a single light on in the old café where everyone used to gather to eat and have activities when it was raining. I'd have to cross through the open to get there, but at least I was wearing a black T-shirt and the yard lights weren't working.

The snap of every dry twig I stepped on seemed to be magnified, and my heart jumped into my throat several times. The last one was so loud I froze, sure Edwards would come racing out guns blazing.

The entire building was screened in but otherwise open to the outdoors. So any little noise I made could potentially be heard by whoever was inside.

When no alarm ensued, I made my way up to the windows in a crouch. The area with all the tables was empty. Moving on, I cautiously peeked into the kitchen.

Chet was pacing back and forth with his phone to his ear. Hands cuffed to the handle of the old industrial stove, Hailey sat on the ground. Eyes wide, and tears tracking down her cheeks, she quietly watched Chet.

That's when it hit me. Not only was she the only woman to capture my goddamn heart, she was likely carrying my child. Because of my stubborn misconceptions, I'd essentially thrown her in the path of Chet the psychopath—putting them both in danger.

My stomach churned at the thought.

I'd fucked up. Bad.

I needed to come up with a plan and quick. Who knew who he was talking to or what he'd set in motion? Sure, I could probably pick him off, but what if I missed?

I'd never been so unsure in my fucking life.

A faint sound in the trees had me turning with my weapon pointed in that direction. Reaper, Joker, Apollo, and Hollywood silently emerged from the wooded edge of the property. Relief bled through me.

I motioned that it was only Chet and Hailey in there as I saw Hacker, Vinny, Soap, and Dice working their way around to the other side of the building.

"While it's only him, I suggest we finish this. We don't know who might be on their way," Reaper whispered next to me. I nodded.

"I'm going to lure him out here. When I do, you and Hollywood go in and get Hailey out of there. She's handcuffed to the stove." I expected them not to like my idea, but I was the president and that was my woman.

"Pres—" Reaper mouthed, wanting to silently argue, but I cut him off with a motion of my hand and a glare. Then I quietly made my way toward the back door. The old metal trash cans were still there from years ago with a small pile of rotting lumber. I thought about tipping them but decided that might be too much. Instead, I grabbed the sturdiest piece of wood from the pile, then scooped up some gravel and tossed it at the door before hiding around the corner of the building.

"What the hell?" I heard him say as the wooden screen door creaked open. Cocky fucker didn't give a single thought to someone having found him so quickly. I watched as he shined a light around the area.

Satisfied with his brief search, he turned to head back inside.

Heart slamming against my rib cage, I hefted the wood in my hand to get a better grip. When he reached for the door, I launched toward him and swung, hitting him in the back. Before he could recover, I took another swing and hit the arm he was holding his weapon with.

The gun fell from his hand, and he spun to face me.

"You!" he snarled. When he lunged at me, I made a wide swipe with the wood, making contact with his ribs. The wood snapped in two, and I tossed it to the side.

"Yeah, me. What are you gonna do about it?" I taunted. He tried to make a dive for his weapon, but I landed an uppercut that snapped his head back. He wiped the back of his hand across his face and stared at the blood on it before smiling like a lunatic. His grin was made garish with the bright-red blood coating his teeth and dripping down his chin.

"You think you can get out of this? My friends are already on their way to pick up your little bitch in there. You can't win this time, Luke." He circled with me, looking for a weakness. He struck out, and his fist connected with my cheek, making me stumble back to catch my footing.

Punches flew, followed by grunts from us both. By then we were both winded.

"How does it feel to know you're gonna lose again? The mighty Luke Matthews. You always thought you were such hot shit. Your entire club is gonna go down for the murder of that little girl." He swung and missed. I fought to keep a cool head when I wanted to go berserk on him.

"I should've beat your ass years ago," I growled as I caught him with a blow to the ribs that knocked the air out of him momentarily.

"But you didn't," he gaspingly taunted as he caught me with a left hook.

"Fucker," I spat with a mouthful of blood.

"You're a pussy, just like your little freak of a brother was. Couldn't handle his alcohol and sure as fuck couldn't handle his blow."

"Leave my brother out of this!" I raged as I whaled on him, and he stumbled backward. Keeping my momentum, I landed one punch after the other.

The last one sent him to his back on the ground.

As I heaved ragged breaths over him, I clenched my fists, wanting to finish him off. He rolled and moaned in the gravel. For good measure, I buried my booted foot in his ribs.

"Why didn't you ever tell them it was me?" he gasped through a groan.

"Because it was your father who showed up on the scene that day. You think he or anyone else would've believed the kid from the wrong side of the tracks over a cop's kid?" I knew I was right. "You were supposed to be his friend. What the fuck happened to you?"

Disgust poured from me as I stared down at the man who had once been my brother's friend. At least he was supposed to be.

"You think I wanted to stay in this shithole town? Become a cop like my ol' man? Hell no! I wanted out! I wanted bigger and better things! But I was railroaded into following in his footsteps. So I made the most of it, and I'm not gonna let some two-bit piece-of-trash wannabe gangster and his whore fuck that up for me." He spat blood on the ground and jumped up at me.

I'd gotten lax, thinking he was beat, and didn't see the knife until it was too late. The shouts from my brothers coincided with the burning pain of the blade sinking into my side. My breath ripped from my lungs at the agony of his last twisting shove.

Shock held me frozen as the world moved in slow motion. I looked at the knife sticking out of my side, then to where Reaper had tackled Chet back to the ground, and finally to the horrified eyes of Hailey where she stood by the edge of the building with her mouth open in shock.

My vision doubled, then cleared, and I dropped to my knees; the pain of the gravel digging into them barely registered. Blood seeped through my clothing to drip on the ground, and I was transfixed by the sight of the growing puddle before I started to fall.

As Apollo laid me down, everything went black.

Chapter
TWENTY-ONE

Hailey

"WHEN IT COMES TO LOVING YOU"—JON LANGSTON

I F SOMEONE HAD TOLD ME I'D FALL MADLY IN LOVE WITH A biker, I would've laughed. Because hello, what a cliche after that show, right? But hell if I hadn't. That's why, when he told me I couldn't be pregnant with his kid, I lost my shit. My feelings were all over the place between the hormones and the fact that I was head over heels for a man who'd told me not to attach feelings to what we had.

Now, if that same person had said I would watch as a madman stabbed the love of my life in the guts, I would've punched them in the throat. Because what a fucked-up thing to say. Yet, there I was, living it.

Once the shock settled, I tried to run to him, but someone with thick tattooed arms held me back. "Let me go!" I screamed as I thrashed to get free.

"Ouch!" The man holding me shouted as my booted foot made contact with his shin. "Goddamn it, woman! You need to stay out of the way so Apollo can help him!"

The fight left me, and I sagged. Thankfully, he didn't let me fall.

"There's so much blood," I sobbed as I watched one of the guys toss a bag to Apollo.

"If anyone can take care of him, it's Apollo," Soap said as he cautiously loosened his grip on me. I didn't care what had happened to Chet by that time. I couldn't have cared less if they filleted him, quite frankly. He was a vile human.

I turned to Hacker and Joker, who had moved up next to us. "He told me he framed you guys for Danielle's murder," I admitted as my shoulders curled in.

"He tried. Little did he know, we caught his destruction of our clubhouse on camera. So even with the evidence he planted, he'll have a hard time getting it to stick. Especially since I got his little minion pulling the bag out of his pocket before he went into Two-Speed's room. His search was bullshit," Hacker assured me with a satisfied grin.

"What are you going to do to him?" I hesitantly questioned as I tried not to watch Apollo working on Luke. If I didn't see all the blood, I could fool myself into believing it wasn't as bad as it looked.

"It's probably best you don't know," Joker said before breaking his gaze from mine and stepping back. He quietly spoke with two of the other guys.

"He was going to sell me," I said. A shudder chased through me at the realization of how close I'd been to having that happen. I wrapped my arms around my middle and fought to not break down in front of the others. I was teetering on the edge of losing my shit.

"Jesus," Soap muttered.

"We need to get Snow out of here before Chet's friends show up. Joker, I need you to pull the SUV up," Reaper announced. "I'm going to wait to see who the mystery guests are."

"But they'll see you!" I said in fear.

"Don't worry. If I don't want to be seen, I won't be." Reaper's ominous announcement sent a chill through me.

"I'm staying with you," Hollywood insisted.

Apollo looked over his shoulder and nodded. He had supplies spread around him that he'd used and discarded. "We need to get the hell out of here and clean up out here," he said as he went back to Luke.

"Already made the call to Venom and the boys. They're on their way," said Vinny in his northeastern accent.

"Wait, what about Luke? Is he going to be okay?" I asked, worry heavy in my tone. The thought of losing him had nausea churning in my guts and tears burning my eyes.

"I've done what I can here. We need to get him back to the infirmary. I think he'll be okay, but I want Angel to take a look at him when they get here. Please tell me he's coming?" Apollo asked as he held Vinny's gaze. Something seemed to pass between them that made me nervous.

Vinny nodded. Reaper backed a dark SUV up to where Luke lay on the ground. They made quick work of loading him up and picking up their trash. During the entire process, Luke didn't regain consciousness once. Several of the guys had dragged Chet off as soon as they'd tackled him. Not my concern.

I'd been angry that they didn't intervene immediately, but one of them had said their prez needed the closure. I hadn't understood what they were talking about, but no closure seemed worth the chance that he might die.

After the way he reacted to the news of my pregnancy, I was actually surprised that he'd come after me. My chest and stomach were in knots. I had no idea where we were, but it would devastate me if he didn't make it. I drew in a deep, unsteady breath.

They had me climb in the backseat of the SUV, and I turned in my seat to reach over to touch him. Despite my angry thoughts as I'd left the club's property, I needed that reassurance that he was there.

Warm.

Breathing.

"He's going to be okay," Apollo quietly murmured. My worried gaze rose from Luke to lock on to his.

My chest ached so badly I was afraid it was caving in on itself. Breathing was a chore. "I hope so."

Luke suddenly groaned as he swung out with one arm. Apollo caught him by the forearm before he could make contact, and tried to calm him down. His blue eyes snapped open, full of panic until they met and held mine.

"Hailey," he whispered before he winced.

With tears in my eyes, I turned further in the seat so I could reach his hand. Though he squeezed mine back, I didn't miss the tremor in his grip. "Don't talk," I begged him as a tear slipped down my cheek.

He gave a slight shake of his head. "I fucked up. I'm s-sorry."

"Shhh." I tried to comfort him by running my free hand along his hair. He seemed to relax, so I kept at it.

The rest of the trip back to their clubhouse was thankfully uneventful.

Within an hour, several men showed up. I had no idea who they were, but there was an odd energy that surrounded them. Not bad, but… strange.

A dark-haired guy they called Angel went into the infirmary with Apollo, and everyone else was made to leave. I wasn't happy about that and was restlessly pacing in the common area. My hands trembled, and I wrapped my arms tightly around myself and tucked them against my sides.

"Hailey?" I turned to see the oldest of the men watching me closely. Hands shoved deep in his pockets, he cocked his head.

"Do I know you?" I asked nervously. He had two piercings on his bottom lip, one on his eyebrow, and a salt-and-pepper beard. A fitted ball cap was turned backward on his head with the letters RBMC embroidered on the back above stormy eyes that seemed to change color as we spoke.

"No."

The men had seemed friendly, but there was something about this guy that made me watch him curiously. He studied me further as I tightened my arms around my middle. It was taking everything I had not to break down. My nostrils fluttered and my bottom lip trembled as I tried my hardest to keep from crying.

The other man had dark hair that flopped over the palest eyes I'd ever seen. Eyes that seemed to stare into my soul. He murmured something to the first guy about "the babies."

"What babies?" I hadn't seen any children since we'd returned. My gaze scanned the room. The older guy shook his head in amazement as he continued watching me.

"Who are you guys?" I asked as I looked from one to the other and over toward the hall where they had taken Luke. The older guy with the chameleon eyes came closer to me, and the other guy watched me quietly.

"I'm Venom. This is Voodoo. Angel is with your man. That's really all that's important right now." I was confused because more than three of them had arrived.

Slowly, he pulled a hand out of his pocket and reached for me. Inside, I wanted to pull away, but something held me rooted to the floor. When his fingertips made contact with my cheek, I sucked in a startled breath.

"He's going to be okay. I promise. You should go clean up and wait for him in his room. Get some rest," he said softly. Languid warmth filled me, and I suddenly relaxed. Why I believed him, I couldn't say, but I did.

"Okay," I breathed out on a sigh as my shoulders dropped and I gave him a tired half smile.

Slowly, I shuffled back to Luke's room. The same place where the day had taken its turn for the worse. Yet none of that seemed to matter as I stripped, showered, dried off, and crawled into his welcoming bed.

As I drifted off to sleep, I rested my hand protectively on my still-flat belly. As I slipped into dreamland, I had a smile on my face and not a worry on my mind.

"Mmm." I tipped my head to allow better access for the kisses that were raining along my neck and shoulder.

"Wake up, baby." The rumble of a familiar voice had me slowly blinking and trying to focus on where I was. Drowsy still, I rolled over, and a sultry grin curled my lips as I saw the sexy bearded man lying next to me.

"What an awesome dream," I murmured as dream-me reached out to stroke the soft beard of the man I'd lost my heart to. "At least dream-you isn't mad at me."

He chuckled. "I wasn't mad at you, Hailey. I was a fucking idiot operating under a foolish misconception. I'll explain it when you're fully awake."

"Mmm, okay. Well, since we're dreaming together, you should make love to me." I gave him a sleepy smile.

"Oh, I should, should I?" he asked with humor in his voice. I nodded decisively.

"Absolutely."

His beard tickled over me, and I gave a shiver and a giggle. He slowly pulled the bedding back to expose me to his heated stare. Leaning over, he pressed a kiss to my abdomen, then raised his deep blue gaze to mine. "Forgive me?"

"Of course. Thank you for saving me," I murmured as my fingers sifted through his soft hair. This was easily one of the best dreams I'd ever had.

"Always. Any time you need rescuing, I'm your man. I just hope there's no need for that ever again."

"Mmm," I replied as I raked my teeth over my bottom lip. Dreams were amazing, and what I really hoped was that I didn't wake up too soon.

The heat of his mouth blew over my skin before his lips drew my nipple in and suckled. Gripping his hair tightly in my grasp, I moaned as he teased first one breast, then the other. My back arched as I tried to get closer.

With each touch, I lost myself to the dream—Luke—happy to leave the worries of the night behind me in my consciousness. His rough hands smoothed over my skin as if he couldn't get enough.

When his thick length slid into my soaking wet core, I gripped his shoulders, threw my head back, and sighed. He sucked on the side of my neck, marking me as his before he thrust deep. That was when I realized I wasn't sleeping.

"Luke!" I gasped, wide-eyed with worry, yet still in a sleepy, lust-induced haze.

He paused with his face buried in my shoulder. "Yeah?" he asked in a strained tone.

"Oh my God! I thought I was dreaming!"

"Well, I'm pretty much a dream come true." He let out a groaning chuckle into my neck as he stroked slowly in and out. Lean muscle bunched under my hands as I wrapped my arms around his torso and held him tight.

"Luke!" I repeated.

"What?" he rasped before lifting his head to look me in the eye.

"You were hurt! I don't know if this is a great idea," I argued, trying to carefully extricate myself.

"It was barely a flesh wound, I promise," he replied through gritted teeth. Not believing a word he was saying, I gave him a side-eye. The bandage on his side didn't have blood seeping through it, but I didn't trust the stubborn man to take care of himself. When he continued to stare intently at me as his hips moved against mine, I couldn't help it—I gave in.

Maybe it had started in my mind as a dream, but it sure as hell ended as the real deal. The man knew how to work what the good Lord gave him. Each thrust had my eyes rolling back in my head and my nails biting into his skin. He was dominant, yet attentive, as he coaxed orgasm after orgasm from my body.

When he rolled us until I was riding him, I braced my hands on his chest. My hair tumbled down over my breasts, leaving my peaks barely showing through the golden strands. As our hips slowly rolled together, he brushed my wayward locks over my shoulder to expose me to his hands. He alternated plucking, twisting, and pinching my nipples before he cupped my breasts and thrust up into me. He went so deep, my eyes fluttered and I tingled head to toe.

The sensations he evoked in me were like nothing I'd experienced before. Not only was he the best I'd ever had, he was like the missing piece of me. He made me feel whole. Complete.

"I'm going to fill this pussy, and I need you to come with me," he demanded.

"I can't," I gasped as my muscles quivered, on the verge of failure. There was no way I could come again.

Yet he proved me wrong.

His palms skimmed down my sides until he controlled the movement of my hips, and I moaned. He worked my body like no other before him. My eyes fell shut as the familiar sensations of a pending orgasm hit me.

"Open your eyes," he insisted in his growly tone, and I immediately did as he said, eyes locked on the midnight blue of his. "I want to see you fall apart as you ride my cock."

A whimper escaped me as I shattered. Before my eyes was a kaleidoscope of color and white flashes of light. Breathing eluded me as I tensed over him. The only thing my body could seem to do was pulse around his shaft until I was a million splintered pieces of ecstasy floating in the night sky. Ever so slowly, I drifted back to Earth and damn near collapsed on top of him.

By the time we were done, we were both breathless and perfectly sweaty. My head hung as I tried to catch my breath.

"Look at me," he said as he gently tipped my jaw in his direction.

"Yeah?" I asked, panting in satisfaction.

"I fucking love you."

My heart tripped and my breath caught as I searched his eyes, trying to read if he truly meant it. What I saw sent butterflies flitting through my stomach. After the way our last interaction in this room had gone, that was the last thing I expected to hear him say.

"Way to be romantic," I finally said as I giggled and stared into his stormy blue gaze. "But I love you too."

He shifted my boneless form over to rest on the cool linens. I whined when he slipped from my body, leaving me pouting.

"Hailey? We're gonna figure all this shit out," he said as he rose up to lean over me and pressed a kiss to my swollen lips.

With heavy-lidded eyes, I raised my hand to cup his face. "Okay."

There were still a few unknowns, but I believed that with the two of us together, anything was possible.

Chapter
TWENTY-TWO

Snow

"HERE WE ARE"—BREAKING BENJAMIN

Venom's boys returned to the clubhouse with Reaper, Hollywood, and Vinny as dawn broke. Hailey was sleeping soundly, and I needed to find out what they'd gathered. My side was a bit sore, but nothing compared to the fiery burst of pain I'd experienced when the knife had sunk deep into muscle. Thanks to Angel's special ability, there was barely a mark where it had sliced through my flesh.

Not everyone in our chapter knew the secrets of the Royal Bastards MC down in Ankeny, but Decker, or Venom as he was known to everyone in his club, had been my friend nearly my entire life. I'd known about his empathic ability since we were pre-teens, but he'd sworn me to secrecy and I never once betrayed his trust. I'd also never tell a soul that his brother, Angel, could heal people, either.

"What did you find out? Did anyone show up?" I spat the questions out to them.

Reaper looked down the hall toward my room before he locked his gaze on mine. "I think we should take this to the chapel."

Understanding, I motioned for everyone to follow me inside the room we held our meetings in, made club decisions, and was essentially the heart of our clubhouse and chapter. Venom fell in step with me, and the rest followed. The members of the RBMC stood behind Venom and leaned against the wall. Voodoo crossed his arms and watched quietly. Despite him being a trusted member of Venom's club, those ice-blue eyes sent a chill through me.

We took our seats, and Reaper spoke up first.

"Between Soap and Blade, they worked their magic and got Chet to talk. What we found out was interesting, but more than that was who showed up."

"Well, don't keep me in suspense," I drily said, impatient for the news.

Hollywood and Reaper shared a concerned glance before they looked to me again. "It was former senator Damon's men."

You could've heard a pin drop. My brothers looked surprised, but Venom's didn't.

"Is there something you know that we don't?" I asked, directing my question to my friend and president of the Ankeny, Iowa Royal Bastards MC.

He pulled off his cap, ran a large hand through his hair, then settled it back on his head.

"Yeah. Unfortunately, I do."

"Care to enlighten us?" I questioned my friend.

"We've connected him to a trafficking and prostitution ring. Initially, we tried to get him arrested, but he's got too many people in his pocket. We know he's involved, but we can't pin it on him because of those connections and we can't get him alone. He was supposed to get caught up in the sting on a private island last month, but somehow he escaped. The man is a snake," Venom snarled.

"Jesus," I muttered.

Reaper cleared his throat.

"We were able to get Chet to admit he was providing drugs to the kids in the area. He was getting them hooked and then taking the ones that wouldn't be missed. He'd been picking them up from here, across the borders into Minnesota, South Dakota, and Nebraska. They were handed off to Damon's men, who we believe transported them to the seller who auctioned them off. Danielle wasn't supposed to be found in the area. Turns out she was sold to a wealthy businessman in Minneapolis. Things 'got out of hand,' and he accidentally killed her. They dumped her back here in an attempt to frame us."

"Oh, and get this—Chet was getting paid by the Triple X Syndicate for the kids," Hacker added. There were a lot of disgruntled murmurs at the table. No one asked if Chet was still alive. Plausible deniability and all.

"That explains how he afforded his lifestyle on the salary of a small-town cop. Investments, my ass. Everyone knows he blew through the money he inherited from his parents," Hollywood spat out. We also knew who the Triple X Syndicate was—well, not their names, because it seemed no one actually *knew* them.

"That also means Senator Damon must be connected to the Triple X Syndicate. You think that's where the drugs are coming from too?" Joker questioned.

"It would make sense," Venom replied.

"Two-Speed has been cleared, right?" Angel asked. I nodded.

"Yes. The security feeds showed everything. He's not here because his mom slipped and broke her ankle, so he's been staying with her to take care of her."

"Sorry about his mom, but good to hear he was cleared," Venom replied.

"Back to former senator Damon. How hard can it be to track down one man? I know you have men as good as Reaper." Reaper coughed and glared. I rolled my eyes and shook my head before I continued. "Why can't you set up a sniper and take him out?"

"Trust me, we've tried. The man knows he's got a target on his back, and he's a pro at keeping himself covered. Doesn't mean we're giving up, but we also didn't know he was tied up with the shit in your neck of the woods," Venom said with a sigh. "We have no idea who all he has in his pockets, but they must be in high places."

"Speaking of, we need to find out which of the cops are dirty, because you know Chet wasn't in this shit alone. He would need someone to help cover his tracks," I added.

"I'll start combing through the GPD officers. We'll figure it out," Hacker insisted.

None of us would've thought Chet or any of the city cops

were capable of this shit. Sure, we knew he was a dickhead and several of them thought their shit didn't stink, but we didn't expect this level of corruption.

"What do you want to do once we ferret them out?" Soap asked.

"I want them gone. Fuck letting the system dole out their justice." My brothers looked at me. Not that we hadn't done illegal as fuck shit, but to take out several of Grantsville's finest was crossing a line we hadn't crossed before. Except this time was different. They were destroying *children*.

"You get a list to me." Venom stared unwaveringly into my gaze. He didn't need to explain what he meant by that. We knew.

After a deep breath, I nodded. "Anyone have a problem with that?" I questioned as I met each of my brother's gazes one at a time. Each of them shook their heads.

"Find them," I told Hacker, who gave me a nod.

"We need to get on the road," Venom said as he stood. I dismissed my brothers. Venom motioned at his to leave the room.

"I can't thank you enough for your help with this," I said when we were alone.

"That's what brothers are for," he replied with a half smile. "I can't believe you're finally settling down. Never thought I'd see the day."

"Neither did I," I admitted with a shake of my head.

"My boys got everything cleaned up out at the old Bible camp," he told me. His chapter of the Royal Bastards owned a crime-scene cleaning business that worked on legitimate jobs and those that required "special handling." In other words, for the right price, they took out the trash for whoever was willing to pay. Obviously, not everyone knew that either. Thankfully, he cut us a friends-and-family deal.

"Thanks. I really appreciate the help."

"You know I'm here for you. You and your brothers helped me and Loralei without question. That's a debt I could never repay. Besides the fact that you're the closest thing I have to a blood brother." His somber words hit home, and my chest ached. All those years ago, he had been stunned to hear Leon had overdosed. Then he was helpful in getting me into the military and stationed with him. Though he said he'd have done it for anyone, I knew it was so he could keep an eye on me because he knew my mental state was fucked up.

"I appreciate that, and you know you're the closest thing I have to a brother too." We both ignored the slight crack in my voice as I said the words.

"Get that list to me, and it will be taken care of," he reiterated as he gripped my shoulder.

"I want them exposed first. There's no way those pieces of shit are going to go out looking like martyrs." My teeth ground as I stared at my friend.

"Understood. Leave it to us. If your boy needs Facet's help to ferret out the weasels, you just let me know."

I nodded.

As silently as they entered town, they left.

A week later, our area exploded with the news of the city's corrupt officers and how they had been mowed down at a meeting gone bad. The evidence all pointed conclusively at the people they were doing their illicit business with, though their identities were left as unknown at this time. Taking on the Triple X Syndicate was more than we could handle.

In reality, they had been snatched up from patrol, their homes, the gym, the bar, and one from our strip club. There were no witnesses, and as far as anyone knew, they were meeting up with their suppliers for Black Night and got double-crossed.

No one would ever know the truth because Venom and his boys were that good.

While I would've loved to have been the one to put a bullet between Chet's eyes, I was simply happy he was gone. Chet had been the one peddling the drugs Leon had overdosed on. The day Leon died, I held the secret in my heart because I knew if I named Chet as the one who was dealing, it would've been brushed under the rug anyway. His father had done it before when he got caught up in trouble. I knew that time wouldn't have been any different.

When I came home from the military to find he had become a police officer, I thought he had outgrown his delinquencies. I'd been so wrong that I was pissed at myself for not seeing it sooner.

"You sure this is what you want to do?" I asked Baker as he and his brother prepared to get in his car after he stopped by to tell me his plans.

"Yeah. I went into law enforcement to make a difference. That the chief of police was in on that bullshit makes me sick. Don't worry, I'm not going to prevent you from keeping shit balanced, but I'm not going to sit by and let my town fall apart because some asshole got greedy." Baker had applied for the chief of police position when it was vacated, and he had been hired damn near on the spot.

We'd been worried about what that could mean for us, but he'd stopped by to tell me that his younger brother had been hired for his old position with the sheriff's department and to introduce us.

"It's the oldest recorded profession, for fuck's sake. If it can be legal in Nevada, there's no reason it shouldn't be okay everywhere. I guess I believe sex workers have a right to work in a safe place. I'd rather see them protected and safe than being taken advantage of and at risk. Unfortunately, brothels aren't an option at this time, or it could be regulated better." Baker's brother shrugged.

"Agreed. Too bad we don't make the laws. We just enforce them." Baker grinned.

"Well, we'll see you around, Baker." He nodded as he climbed into his cruiser, and he waved his hand on his way out of the gate.

Vinny and Reaper remained silent as they continued to have my back until Baker was out of sight.

"You really think this is a good thing?" Vinny asked in his rumbling New York City accent.

"I hope so," I replied with a sigh. Feeling every minute of my thirty-eight years, I pulled on my helmet and swung my leg over my bike. After settling in the seat, I secured the buckle under my chin and pulled on my gloves.

"Tell Hailey I said hello," Vinny said with a grin.

"Steph wants to have you both over for dinner this weekend," Reaper added as he mounted up on his bike too.

"I'll talk to Hailey. Somehow I doubt she would have a problem with that." I smirked, because Hailey's appetite had significantly increased. The chance to eat Steph's cooking wasn't one any of us wanted to pass up. Since Hailey's appetite had kicked in, I was freaking having sympathy cravings with her. If I didn't add a little extra time to my workout, I was going to end up with a potbelly.

"Catch you later, Vin," I told him before I started my bike. Reaper and I pulled out of the lot, and the prospect closed the gate. We parted with a nod as we passed Reaper's driveway, and I continued home. Hailey should be off work and at the house. Despite my urging, she refused to take time off after what had happened.

It didn't take long for me to park my bike in the garage next to her car. When I went inside, the scent of Italian cooking hit me, and my stomach rumbled. If I wasn't mistaken, that was garlic bread I smelled.

"Hailey?" I called out when she wasn't in the kitchen. As I listened for her reply, I shrugged out of my cut and hung it in the coat closet, then wandered through the house with a frown. Nervous after the ordeal we'd recently experienced, I pulled my pistol from my holster. She wasn't in the living room, nor the bedroom. A rustling in the spare bedroom had me cautiously pushing the door open. What I saw had me smiling as I returned my pistol to its home at my back.

Blonde hair piled up in some kind of wild bun; tendrils of gold escaped and teased her neck. A long shirt that looked suspiciously like one of my old T-shirts was like a dress on her over her leggings. She was dancing and softly humming as she rolled a mint-green paint on the walls.

"Hailey?" I repeated, but she didn't respond, she simply kept painting as her hips swayed. I approached her and cautiously tapped her shoulder.

She shrieked, and the paint roller swung around, catching me upside the head with a splat.

"Oh my God! I'm so sorry," she cried out with wide eyes as she pulled out one of her earbuds. After setting the roller in the paint tray, she lifted my holey shirt at the hem and attempted to wipe the side of my head. The expression on her beautiful face was comical, and I couldn't help but laugh.

By then she was looking at me like I'd lost my mind. At least until I scooped her up and rubbed the side of my face on her and smeared the soft green color on her cheek.

"Luke!" she chastised as I laughed. Unable to hold back her own smile, she grinned at me with her matching green face. "Why did you do that?"

"I figured it was only fair." Then I quickly sobered. "Are you supposed to be painting? Is that dangerous to the baby? Shit! Come on, let's get you in the shower and washed off."

Not wasting a moment, I scooped her up and raced to the bathroom, ignoring her protestations. Once I set her on her feet, I whipped her clothes off and then mine before starting the shower.

"How much time before supper is ready?" I asked. She glanced at her phone, which I had caught before it fell out of her bra and had set on the counter.

"Not long," she replied with a smirk as she stood there naked and laughing.

"Get in," I instructed with a smack to her perfectly shaped ass. She'd been bitching that it was already getting bigger from the pregnancy. If it was, I didn't care. She was beautiful regardless of the size of her ass. Be it small, big, tiny, or ginormous, I loved it because it was on her. Just like every other feature that made her who she was.

Walking out to the kitchen, I turned off the alfredo sauce she had lightly simmering. Then I pulled out the garlic bread and set it on the stovetop. The pasta was already strained and in the pot with a lid on it.

Not wasting any more time, I returned to the bathroom. Her perfect shape was an abstract masterpiece through the rippled glass of the shower door.

As I opened the door, she glanced my way and my breath caught. I'd never seen a woman more beautiful in all my life. A happy smile lifted my lips. She had finished rinsing the shampoo out of her hair, and I chuckled at the mint-green paint still on the side of her nose.

"What's so funny now?" she asked with a soft curve of her lips.

Wetting my hand, I scrubbed her clean. "Nothing. You had a bit of paint you missed."

"Have you looked in the mirror?"

"Oh, I'm sure I'm a mess. Wonder whose fault that is?"

"Yours. You startled me," she replied matter-of-factly.

A chortle of laughter escaped, causing me to snort as I switched places with her so I could try to get the paint off my face and out of my hair. I made quick work of it, because I had other plans before we ate.

First, I framed her wet face with my hands and pressed a chaste kiss to her perfect lips. "I love you, beautiful."

"I love you too," she murmured with a soft smile and water-spiked lashes.

As I stared at her beauty, I squeezed the water out of my hair, slicked it back, then wiped the excess off my face. Before she could get out of the shower, I walked toward her until her back was pressed to the tile wall. Her teeth raked over her bottom lip as her gray eyes darkened. Caging her in, I braced my arms on either side of her.

"I missed you today," I murmured before tilting my head to capture her kiss and claiming it as my own. As far as I was concerned, I owned all her kisses until the day I died. Except for the ones she would bestow on our children.

"Did you?" she asked in a breathy voice when we broke apart. Her lips skimmed mine as she spoke, causing me to groan before I kissed her deeply, savagely, claiming her very soul with my actions.

"What do you think?" I asked once I freed her kiss-swollen lips with one last suckle.

"I'd say I believe you," she answered in a husky tone.

"Good, because I miss you every day," I murmured as I cupped her ass, hefted her up, and she wrapped her legs around my waist at the same time I lined up and drove inside her. No matter how many times we joined, it always felt like the first time—each encounter better than the last.

"Oh, fuck," she gasped as I withdrew and plunged in again.

The steam from the hot water surrounded us as I tasted the skin of her neck, and she tangled her fingers in my hair to hold me to her. "Before you know it, we won't be able to do it like this," she whispered as I steadily filled her tight pussy with my cock.

"Yeah? Well, then I guess we'll have to switch to this," I said as I set her legs down, withdrew, much to her disappointment, and spun her around. "Hands on the wall."

She obeyed without question, and I wondered how I'd gotten so lucky that night in Kansas City. I wrapped my fingers around her hips and pulled gently to get her to stick that ass out for me. Then I slowly stroked through her wetness until the tip of my aching cock found its way home.

"Goddamn, baby. I swear to Christ you feel better each time."

"Enough talk. Fuck me already," she tossed out. A wicked grin lifted the corners of my mouth as I gave her what she wanted. When I could feel my balls tighten and the base of my spine sent fire licking up my back, I circled her puckered hole with my thumb before slowly pushing the end through. For a second she froze and tensed up. But it wasn't long before she relaxed and pushed back into me as I drove forward.

"Like that?" I asked as I gave her what I knew she wanted and rammed my hard shaft into her again and again until she babbled nonsensically.

"God, yes," she panted out as her hands slipped on the wall before she slapped them back in place.

"This pussy feels so goddamn good. Who does it belong to?" I demanded.

All I got out of her was a garbled moan.

"Hailey…," I warned. When she huffed but didn't answer and tried to get me deeper, I stopped all movement.

"Luke," she whined.

Using one hand, I reached up and wrapped her honey-gold locks in my hand before I tugged her head back. Then I leaned forward and whispered in her ear. "If you want me to fuck you,

you tell me whose tight, wet cunt this is," I ground out as I gave her a teasing stroke with both my cock and my thumb.

A gasp left her lips. My fingers clutched her hair tighter. "Answer me."

"You! It's yours!" she finally burst out as she intentionally tightened her sheath around my cock.

"Damn right it is," I growled out. "This is my ass too, isn't it?"

I knew what buttons to push to get her to come, and that was one of them. Telling her what to do, talking dirty to her, and giving it to her hard were guaranteed to make her not only lose her mind but come almost immediately. Several strokes in and I noticed her pussy began to tighten. Working her ass with my thumb and pounding her hot, wet cunt with my cock, it didn't take long before she was screaming my name, and she clenched around me, triggering my release.

Never before her had I come so violently it left me disoriented. But I sure as hell did with her sheath clutching me tightly.

When we could both breathe, I loosened my hold on her hair and brought her back to my front. Gently, I kissed the sexy slope of her shoulder, up her neck, and behind her ear. One hand splayed on her abdomen and the other over her chest, I quietly held her.

"I never thought I'd find someone that made me feel what you do," I murmured against the side of her head. "The thought of losing you causes me physical pain. I'm so sorry I treated you like shit when you told me you were pregnant."

Her head dropped back to my shoulder as she looked up at me. "You've apologized a million times. It's not necessary. If I were in your shoes and thought I wasn't capable of having children, I would've been pissed if someone I barely knew told me she was pregnant. The only thing I wish is that you had taken a few minutes to talk to me that day."

"But that's why I hate that I treated you that way—I did know you. I knew your heart and knew your soul. You are a good person, Hailey. I shouldn't have doubted that."

"Well, I tell you what," she whispered with a smirk as she spun in my hold and draped her arms over my shoulders. "You can spend the rest of my pregnancy making it up to me."

"Oh yeah? How's that?" I asked as I held back my smile.

"Endless orgasms should do it," she replied with an impish grin that she tried to subdue by biting her lip.

"Oh is that right?" I asked as I nipped her neck before I growled and teased her with playful bites. Her laughing squeals were music to my ears.

"Yep," she said between giggles as she squirmed in my arms and the water began to cool.

"Well, I don't think I can do that," I announced.

Her eyes widened and her laughter died off. "Huh?"

"I'm pretty sure I'll need a lifetime of your orgasms to feel I've been redeemed." My tongue trailed up the side of her neck before I placed a kiss on her jaw. A soft sigh fell from her lips.

"I think I can work with that," she drawled languidly as I cupped her ass and held her flush to my front.

"Good. Now let's go eat before I toss you on that bed and ravage you again."

"Promises, promises," she teased.

I gave her ass a loud smack, causing a sharp inhale. "Let's dry off and eat."

We did just that but sat naked eating chicken alfredo before we were back at each other. The moon was high in the sky before we drifted off to sleep in each other's arms.

I'd always hated the word addiction, but there wasn't a better way to describe my need for her. Her laughter, her smiles, her love—I was addicted to it all.

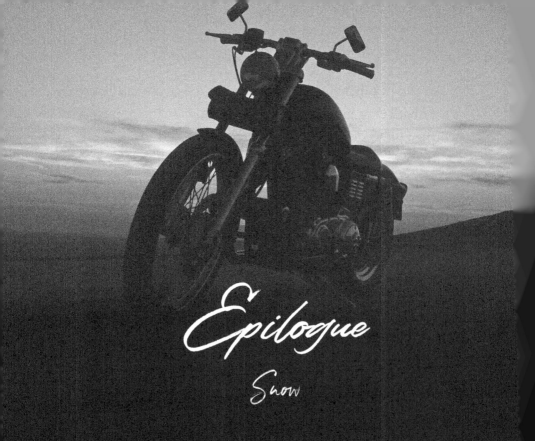

Epilogue

Snow

A CONTINUOUS BUMPING WOKE ME UP, AND AT FIRST, I thought it might be my phone vibrating, though I didn't know why it would be in the bed. Disoriented, I lifted my head and glanced around. The house was silent, light was barely filtering around the blinds and curtains as dawn made its sleepy arrival on the day.

A naked, warm body was curled around mine that smelled of green apples and some kind of floral mix. It was Hailey's favorite lotion that she put on every night before bed. Her belly was pressed to my side and she had one leg hooked over mine while my chest pillowed her head. The feeling hit me again, and I realized it was her stomach—or more accurately, our son.

"You're gonna wake up your mother, kiddo," I said to the curve of her abdomen as I wrapped an arm around her. She'd been restless as hell last night, and I really didn't feel like either of us slept much.

"He doesn't care," she sleepily muttered before lifting her head and wiping her mouth.

"Did you just drool all over me?" I asked my heavy-lidded wife, who frowned, looked at my chest where I could see a small puddle, and had the audacity to look me square in the eye and lie to me.

"Nope."

"Oh, really?" I drawled then pointed at my chest. "Then what's that?"

"A really sexy chest," she murmured as she gave me a sleepy smile, causing me to laugh.

"Covered in drool," I added.

She sighed. "Well, if your bed was more comfortable, I wouldn't have to use you as a pillow."

Her shrug was completely unapologetic.

"Well, your bed is only a queen, so we're stuck with mine. The way you alternate between starfishing and sleeping on top of me, I'd be right on the edge of a queen—if not the floor," I explained for the hundredth time to her. No matter how many times I said it, she refused to admit she was a bed hog.

"We should get a new bed," she suggested through a yawn. Her body arched as she stretched.

"There's nothing wrong with this one," I argued with a laugh and a shake of my head.

"It's hard," she grumbled.

Waking up further, she sat up and straddled me. "Mmm, so are you. What should we do about that?"

My morning wood was perfectly happy with that situation, and my hips reflexively lifted to put pressure on it. When she wiggled until I could feel her hot, wet pussy sliding up and down my length as it rested between us, I groaned.

"Don't start something you can't finish, baby."

"Oh, I have every intention of—" That was all she got out before the two of us and the bed were soaked. Her hand went to her abdomen as she winced.

"Was that—" I started, but she doubled over and gasped. Her wide-eyed gaze was full of pain.

"Shit!" I said as I carefully lifted her and set her next to me. "I'll be right back!"

I took the quickest shower known to man before I was back in front of her, helping her get dressed.

A keening cry escaped her as she doubled over and held her stomach.

"Jesus, how did this come on so fast?" she asked between panted breaths.

"I have a feeling this has been going on for a while. Likely all night, which is why we slept so shitty." Kneeling at her feet, I slipped her slides on. Then I grabbed the bag she'd packed weeks ago. It had been alternating between the back seat of my truck and sitting on our dresser since then. We'd made several trips to the hospital only to be turned away because it was a false alarm.

She bent over several times on the way to my truck and tried to breathe through her contractions. The leggings I'd put on her were wet by the time we made it to the garage.

"What the hell? Doesn't that stuff stop at some point?" I questioned with eyes wide in shock.

"I have no idea! This is my first kid too!" she ground out, and I paused. My hands framed her face.

"Look at me, baby," I instructed. Slowly, her tear-filled gaze locked with mine. "We've got this. I'll be with you every step of the way. Okay?"

With a sniffle, she nodded. I tossed the waterproof mattress pad we'd picked up for just such an event onto the seat.

Another contraction hit her as she was climbing in, and I glanced at my watch. *Shit*. They were coming closer each time.

Placing my hand on her seat, I looked over my shoulder and backed us out of the garage. Within seconds I was tearing down the road toward the hospital. On the way, I called Vinny. With each ring, my anxiety ratcheted up a notch. My hand nervously scrubbed my mouth and chin. My beard was likely a hot mass. Finally, he answered, and I let out the breath I didn't know I'd been holding.

"Hailey's in labor," I told him. "Let everyone know."

"I got you, brother," he said, then hung up. Within minutes everyone in our chapter, and likely chapters throughout the nation, would know.

Telephone, tell-a-Demented-Son.

"Oh my God! Hurry!" she cried out as I raced through the streets of Grantsville.

"I'm trying, baby. Christ, I'm trying."

We skidded to a stop in front of the hospital, and I helped her down from the still-running truck. I wanted to carry her, but she swatted me away. The budding spring flowers in front of the hospital carried the scent of spring on the air. It wasn't lost on me that my son would be born in a time of rebirth as green slowly spread through the rolling hills of our area.

No one was at the front desk, and I cussed under my breath as we kept going to the elevator. As we waited for it to arrive, she doubled over. "Oh God, Luke! I think he's coming."

"I know, baby; we're almost there."

"No! I mean he's coming *out!*"

"What?" I practically shrieked as I stared at her while I repeatedly banged on the up button.

Someone must've heard us because a woman in blue scrubs came running with a wheelchair. "Ma'am! Here!" She quickly got Hailey situated, but she couldn't sit. She was on one hip and she clutched one arm of the wheelchair and leaned over it.

The fucking elevator finally opened, and we rushed in, thankful no one was getting off. The nurse asked our names, then called someone from the little black box on her shirt. "Incoming!" was all she called out.

The three of us burst out as soon as the doors opened, and Hailey lifted one foot to the seat as she spread her knees.

"Get these pants off me!" She was franticly pulling at the waistband.

"Almost there," the nurse cheerily announced. When her gaze hit mine, I could tell she was worried too, but we both stayed silent.

As we passed the nurse's station, another nurse called out from a doorway. We headed that way, and the two nurses helped Hailey maneuver from the wheelchair to the bed as I stood there feeling helpless as fuck. They made quick work of her clothes;

switching them for a gown. As they did, I caught a glimpse of a dark area between Hailey's legs.

There's no way.

"Get Dr. Moser on the phone!" one of them shouted to a third woman in scrubs who slid to the doorway. "She's crowning!"

That had the third nurse, or whatever she was, scrambling. Hell, in my mind anyone in scrubs was a nurse. I didn't really care as long as they took care of my ol' lady and my son.

Then I paused. "Wait. Crowning?"

My harried gaze caught one of the nurse's. "Yes, Mr. Matthews. Your baby is on his way, and he's in a hurry, it would appear."

"You think?" I shouted, heart slamming against my ribs and stomach bottoming out.

Everything was a blur as I clutched Hailey's hand and rattled off the most encouraging words I could think of. Sweat plastered her hair to the sides of her reddened face, but she was a trooper. Other than grunts through clenched teeth, she didn't scream once.

The doctor was still pulling on light blue hospital scrubs as she rushed into the room in time to catch my baby like a motherfucking football. "Whoa! You don't waste time, Ms. Monroe!" the doctor said as she handed my son off to a nurse who laid him on Hailey's bare chest.

Tears burst from her eyes, and she ugly cried like a champ. "Oh my God, Luke. He's here. Isn't he beautiful?" She took her loving gaze from our wrinkled, white-coated son for the briefest second to look eagerly at my wondrous expression. I'd never seen something like what just happened. I was pretty sure I was a little in shock.

"He's absolutely the most precious thing I've ever seen," I murmured as I shook off my shocked stupor and leaned down to place a soft kiss on both his head and his mother's. Fuck the cheesy white shit, that was my son. A miracle if I'd ever seen one. A gift that I once thought I would never want but now couldn't be happier. Love blossomed in my heart.

If I thought my love for Hailey was a wonder, the emotions I carried in my heart for this tiny human were mind-blowing. In that split second, I knew I'd lay down my life for them. I'd slay dragons and bad guys if it meant they stayed forever safe. My club was my family, but these two were my world.

"Dad?" the doctor asked as she held out surgical scissors and motioned to the cord still connecting our son to his mother. Slightly dazed, I took it and placed it over the spot they pointed out between two clamps. It took me a moment, but finally, our son was officially out in the world—the physical connection to his mother severed. But if the expression on her face as she reverently touched each tiny finger, the little ear, and rounded cheek was any indication, there would always be a special bond that nothing could sever.

By the time it was said and done, and we were sitting in the quiet room that had recently been a bustling madhouse, my brothers started to peek their heads in.

"The nurse said you might not want to see us," Joker said with a frown. "I got elected to ask."

Vinny, Reaper, Hollywood, Hacker, Apollo, and the rest were all peeking around each other to see inside the room. I cast a questioning glance at Hailey, who nodded with a serene smile and quietly ended her call with her friend Justine. Our son rested his small head on her chest with his little butt over her arm. Wrapped up and wearing a little tiny beanie, he slept peacefully against the soft skin of his mother.

"It's okay," I told him, and their ol' ladies, who must've been hidden behind all their bulk, pushed their way to the front. Steph, Becca, Kassie, and Sera all stood with hands over their mouths as they made goo-goo eyes at the newest Matthews to enter the world.

"Oh my God, he's beautiful!" They each took turns exclaiming. I'd be lying if my chest didn't puff a little in pride.

The nurse came in to assess Hailey, and everyone said their goodbyes.

"Congrats again, boss man," Soap said, as he was the last one heading out the door. "The little prince has big shoes to fill, but he's in good hands."

With a wave, he softly closed the door.

"Blessed silence. Finally," I muttered to Hailey's chuckle. I scooped up my son as the nurse did her assessments and spoke quietly with Hailey. I didn't hear a thing they said because I was too transfixed on the perfect little features of my son.

My son.

Two words I never thought I'd say. Two words I thought I never wanted to say. I couldn't have been more wrong. He wrinkled his nose as a huge yawn stretched his tiny toothless mouth wide. Slowly, he blinked before his dark blue eyes peeked, then a few more blinks and they were staring at me.

"It's you and me, kid. It's our job to watch over your mom

and keep her safe. No one messes with her, and anyone who tries gets a pop in the kisser," I said as I gently used his tiny fist and pretended he was boxing.

I was vaguely aware of the nurse and Hailey trying to keep their laughter quiet. "They can laugh all they want, but you and I, we got each other's backs. Right?"

"Right," I said in a high-pitched little voice as if he was answering. That time, Hailey couldn't hold in her snort of laughter, and I shot her a mock-glower.

"Do you mind? My son and I are having a serious conversation here," I loftily announced with a cocked brow.

"Oh, is that right?" she asked with a huge smile. Despite damn near giving birth in the hallway of the hospital, she looked beautiful. My heart was full as I took in her still damp tendrils that stuck to her temples and forehead.

"Yes. Now shush, woman."

"Woman?"

"Yes. *My* woman."

Another snort. I cast her another playful glare.

"Sooooo… Looks like we're getting a new bed, huh?" she asked with a wide mischievous grin.

"It would appear so," I said with a matching smile as I dropped my gaze to our son.

"You just made your mother doubly happy today," I told him.

I swear he winked at me.

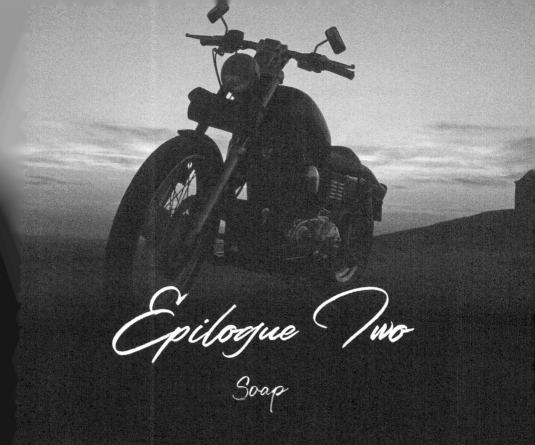

Epilogue Two

Soap

REAPER AND THE BOYS THAT HAD FAMILIES WENT HOME AFTER we left the hospital. Me, Blue, Apollo, and the two prospects came back to the clubhouse. We racked the balls on the felt and prepared to shoot a game of pool.

"Hit the tunes, prospect!" I called out as I lifted my beer to my lips.

Tash and her friend Hattie came in, and I did my best not to stare. Her sidelong gaze caught mine as she passed, but she didn't stop. We'd both been skating around whatever the sexual tension was, but that's all it could ever be. God knew that I wasn't fit company for any woman. The things that were in my head would've scarred a lesser man so bad that he'd likely be in a nut hut the rest of his life.

Blue and I flipped a coin to see who broke. When I uncovered the quarter on the back of my hand, I looked up at him.

"You break," I told him as my attention briefly darted over to where Tash sat at the bar.

He gave me a salute. "Be prepared to lose your ass," he said with a cocky grin.

As I stood with both hands resting on the top of my cue, I tried to ignore Tash's covert glances. The problem was, she was my flame and I was her stupid, helpless moth. Because I knew I'd get burned if I got too close, but her lure was so powerful, I almost wanted to risk it.

"Fuck," I muttered under my breath as I saw her get off her stool and head my way.

"Hey, Soap," she said, and the soft lilt of her voice washed over me like warm honey. Her tits were perky, and her Shamrock T-shirt had been cut off at the bottom and at the neck to reveal her ample cleavage. Despite my threats to them, my traitorous eyes stared. It pissed me off that Zena had let Tash start dancing. It had been bad enough when she waitressed. The groping hands of the customers had me seeing red. Now that she was dancing, it was worse.

"Hey," I grumbled before reaching for my beer.

It all seemed like it happened in slow motion. My bottle shattered in my hand, beer splattering everywhere. Blue's eyes went wide, and he glanced down at the red that spread from a hole in his chest before he dropped to the ground. The whiz and crash of shit breaking spurred me into action.

I dove at Tash, where she stood screaming and frozen in place. Protecting her from the fall, I took the brunt of the impact as I yelled for my brothers and the prospects to get down. As soon as we were down, I rolled to protect Tash with my body.

"Goddamn it!" I shouted as shit around us was shredded, one bullet at a time. By the time the cacophony of sound stopped, the silence seemed deafening. Smoke and dust filled the air. The clubhouse was a disaster area, and what seemed like a million holes in the front wall seemed to glitter as the blinding spring sun shone through them.

The sound of groans and shit being pushed aside surrounded me. I had no idea if it had been there all along or if it was just sifting through my consciousness.

"Who all is here?" Apollo shouted out before he coughed from the dusty debris floating in the air.

"We're over here! Check Blue! He was hit!" I called out.

"Tash, let's get you up and make sure I didn't break anything," I said as I pushed her hair back. That's when I saw the blood starting to pool beneath her.

"No," I gasped. "No! No, no, no, no, no. Tash." I gently shook her and tapped her soft cheek. Her lashes didn't so much as flutter. Quickly, I rolled her to see where the blood was coming from. Then I slammed my hand over the bullet hole in her back. My other hand grabbed my shirt and dragged it over my head.

"He's gone," Apollo said from the other side of the pool table before I saw him scramble around to where I crouched over Tash. "What have we got?" he asked in a no-nonsense tone as he assessed the damage.

"Bullet to the back," I choked out.

"Fuck," he muttered as he checked for a pulse. Something

I had been too afraid to do as I held my wadded-up shirt to the wound on her back. His pained gaze hit mine.

"No. Goddamn it! No! Don't you fucking say it!" I roared at my friend and brother.

A pained cry pierced the air as I lost the last shred of humanity I had left.

They might've called me Soap, but I was a soulless husk. I was going to find out who had done this to us, and I would rip them apart limb from limb.

Because I was a demon bent on revenge, hiding in a man's body.

The End.

Look for Soap's story coming soon.

Acknowledgements

Though this book wasn't dedicated to you, I thank you. You read this book and now here you are—at the end and into the boring, weird stuff. Kudos to you, now hang on for the rest of the ride.

Once upon a time there was a girl who made up stories in her head. The books she read were never written the way they were supposed to because she imagined them playing out differently. Yet she read—no, she devoured—books. They became her inspiration, her escape, her dreams, and her adventure. That girl was me. I know, you're surprised, right?

That's why I dedicated this book to the non-believers. For all of you who think dreams and wishes are foolish, I present my twenty-four standalone book. That's not including the couple that were in anthologies and are maybe chilling on my laptop waiting to either be extended or released to the masses as is. To those of you who dream, you'll get there.

Thank you to everyone who believed in me. Thank you to everyone who encouraged me. Thank you to everyone who held me up when I wanted to fall. And thank you to those of you who keep reading everything I write.

If this is my first book you've read, you may not know who he is, but a huge thank you goes out to **PSH**, my very own Porn Star Hubby (if you ever meet me, or friend me on social media, ask me to tell you the story). You're the best book schlepper, one man cheerleading squad, and pimp-er of my books that ever walked the earth. Love you bunches.

To my squad: **Pam**, **Kristin**, **Brenda**, **Lisa** for being my betas and letting me bounce ideas off you at all hours of the night. I seriously couldn't do this without you. YOU ARE AWESOME!

Thank you to **Kristine's Street Team**! Y'all are amazing! I cannot thank you enough for your time and your efforts in sharing my book babies with the masses! Hugs and kisses!

Penny. Once upon a time there was a girl who didn't believe in herself. Then came a red-headed girl that smacked the first girl upside the head and said, "You can do this!" Thank you for believing in me enough for both of us in the beginning and always. You are never surprised at my success and *that* is humbling.

Lisa and **Brenda**, we met through our love of books. You invited me to join you at a book signing when I had no idea what they were. I had two books out still didn't really know what I was doing. Your support, advice, and friendship have been priceless. I love you guys! Thank you for loving the fact that my mind is always moving and my characters take over at times.

Clarise, you brought my visions to life with this cover! With it, we came full circle. You designed my first twelve books and some in between. To bring it back to that first series was like coming home. It turned out as beautiful as the originals—if not more so.

Golden, this image of Scott was PERFECT for Snow. You have an eye for exactly what I'm looking for (hence all the images of yours I have just waiting for their stories to be told hahahaha!) Thank you.

Scott, thank you for gracing the cover of Snow. You were exactly what I envisioned for him. Being able to finally meet you in person at TNTNYC was awesome! And by the way, you're *way* taller than I imagined you were. Thanks for being so down to earth and cool—even when I let my dorky side slip when I kept writing your last name wrong (repeatedly!) because I was trying to act calm when inside I was all "OMG Scott Benton is talking to me like a normal-ass person! He's on my cover and I'm *talking* to him!" Oh, and thanks for being super awesome with PSH. He thinks your a pretty great guy too. LOL.

Stacey of **Champagne Book Design**, you are and forever will be a goddess! We *finally* got to meet at Shameless! Squeeeee! What I wouldn't have given to join you for those margaritas you posted. LOL. Thank you for making each book better and more beautiful than the last. Did you ever think we'd have made this many pretties together?

The ladies of **Kristine's Krazy Fangirls**, y'all are the best. You're the lovers of my books, the ones that I share my funny stories with, the ones who cheer me on when I'm struggling with a book I promised you, and I love you all to pieces! (((BIG HUGS)))! I can't thank you enough for your comments, your support, and your love of all things books. Come join us if you're not part of the group www.facebook.com/groups/kristineskrazyfangirls

Often, I try to spin the military into my books. This is for many reasons. Because of those reasons, my last, but never least, is a massive thank you to America's servicemen and women who protect our freedom on a daily basis. They do their duty, leaving their families for weeks, months, and years at a time, without asking for praise or thanks. I would also like to remind the readers that not all combat injuries are visible, nor do they heal easily. These silent, wicked injuries wreak havoc on their minds and hearts while we go about our days completely oblivious. Thank you all for your service.

Other Books

Demented Sons MC Series - Iowa
Colton's Salvation
Mason's Resolution
Erik's Absolution
Kayde's Temptation
Snow's Addiction

Straight Wicked Series
Make Music With Me
Snare My Heart
No Treble Allowed
String Me Up

Demented Sons MC Series - Texas
Lock and Load
Styx and Stones
Smoke and Mirrors
Jax and Jokers
Got Your Six (Formerly in Remember Ryan Anthology - Coming Soon!)

RBMC - Ankeny Iowa
Voodoo
Angel
A Very Venom Christmas
Chains
Haunting Ghost
Phoenix (Coming Soon!)
Blade (Coming Soon!)
Sabre (Coming Soon!)

The Iced Series
Hooking
Tripping
Roughing
Holding (Coming Soon!)

Heels, Rhymes, & Nursery Crimes
Roses Are Red (RBMC connection)
Violets Are Blue (Coming Soon!)

Pinched and Cuffed Duet with M. Merin
The Weight of Honor
The Weight of Blood (by M. Merin)

About the Author

Kristine Allen lives in beautiful Central Texas with her adoring husband. They have four brilliant, wacky, and wonderful children. She is surrounded by twenty-six acres, where her five horses, five dogs, and six cats run the place. She's a hockey addict and feeds that addiction with season tickets to the Texas Stars. Kristine realized her dream of becoming a contemporary romance author after years of reading books like they were going out of style and having her own stories running rampant through her head. She works as a night shift nurse, but in stolen moments, taps out ideas and storylines until they culminate in characters and plots that pull her readers in and keep them entranced for hours.

Reviews are the life blood of an indie author. If you enjoyed this story, please consider leaving a review on the sales channel of your choice, bookbub.com, goodreads.com, allauthor.com, or your review platform of choice, to share your experience with other interested readers. Thank you! <3

Follow Kristine on:

Facebook www.facebook.com/kristineallenauthor

Instagram www.instagram.com/_jessica_is_kristine.allen_

Twitter @KAllenAuthor

TikTok: vm.tiktok.com/ZMebdkNpS

All Author www.kristineallen.allauthor.com

BookBub www.bookbub.com/authors/kristine-allen

Goodreads www.goodreads.com/kristineallenauthor

Webpage www.kristineallenauthor.com

Made in the USA
Middletown, DE
07 May 2023

30002863R00130